The House at the Top Of The Bottoms

A boy's life during the Great Depression

Best wishes Shelley! to you were one of my brightest students. Congratulations for dedicating your life to the arts. Mike Lockett 2022

The House at the Top Of The Bottoms

A boy's life during the Great Depression

Michael L. Lockett

Parkhurst Brothers Publishers

MARION, MICHIGAN

www.parkhurstbrothers.com

Consumers may order Parkhurst Brothers books from their favorite online or bricks-and-mortar booksellers, expecting prompt delivery. Parkhurst Brothers books are distributed to the trade through the Chicago Distribution Center. Trade and library orders may be placed through Ingram Book Company, Baker & Taylor, Follett Library Resources and other book industry wholesalers. To order from Chicago Distribution Center, phone 1-800-621-2736 or fax to 800-621-8476. Copies of this and other Parkhurst Brothers Publishers titles are available to organizations and corporations for purchase in quantity by contacting Special Sales Department at our home office location, listed on our web site. Manuscript submission guidelines for this publishing company are available at our web site.

Printed in the United States of America

First Edition, September, 2021
Printing history: 2021 2022 2022 8 7 6 5 4 3 2 1

Library Cataloging Data
  1.   Author–Lockett, Michael, American storyteller and author
  2.   Subject–Fiction, Americana
  3.   Subject–YA Fiction
  2020-trade paperback and e-book

ISBN: Trade Paperback   978-1-62491-151-4
ISBN: e-book   978-1-62491-152-1

Cover and Interior design by   Linda D. Parkhurst, Ph.D.
Principal Editing by   Richard Culbertson
Acquired for Parkhurst Brothers Publishers by   Ted Parkhurst
Cover and Interior Art Adapted from Lockett Family Photos.

092021

Dedication and Acknowledgment

THIS BOOK IS DEDICATED TO MY FAMILY AND ALL OF MY FRIENDS in education from thirty-three years working in schools. Special gratitude is expressed to my wife, Becky, may she rest in peace. Becky and our two sons, Michael and Mark listened to revision after revision. Appreciation goes to my father and mother, Bobby and Peggy Lockett. They always believed in me, including in my dreams to write for children. Thanks to my in-laws, Stanley and Mary Matsick, for sharing stories from their childhood which made this story more historically accurate. Finally, I wish to also acknowledge the time spent by teachers who tested this novel with their students.

Contents

RAILS NORTHWARD

THE SOUND OF THE STEEL WHEELS COULD BE HEARD squealing and grinding again and again as the train moved over the iron rails. Clickety-clack, clickety-clack, over and over again, like the rhythm of a song. The sound was only broken by an occasional clickety-clickety-clickety-clickety where the tracks passed over a crossing at a highway or a bridge. I had only been on the train with my family for a short time, but I already knew where everything on the train was from the engine clear back to the caboose. We had left Coalton, Illinois after saying goodbye to Grandma and her house at the top of the bottoms and were about halfway to Chicago. From there, the train would make a stop at Chicago Union Station and then sweep toward the northwest, taking us toward north central Wisconsin.

"Michael Polonec," I heard a stern voice over the music the rails were singing to me. It was Momma, seated across the aisle from me in the middle of the car. "Go find out where Sissy went."

I already knew, but went anyway to look at the back of the car where the bathrooms were. Just a few minutes earlier, I had shown Melissa, my eight-year-old sister, a great discovery. When you flushed the toilet, you could see the tracks below the train! Sissy, as all of us called her, hadn't believed me when I told her where the toilet emptied and had gone to see for herself. I had shown her how to pull the wooden handle attached to a chain that hung from the porcelain tank on the wall. On pulling the handle, the bottom of the toilet opened up and water drained from the tank to rinse out the pot, causing a rush of cold air to come up from the opening, freshening the smell of the bathroom. Below, the tracks were clearly visible. Then, just as fast, the opening closed up again, making you wonder if you had imagined it.

I knocked on the door before opening it, just in case Sissy was using the pot for real. I opened the door to the bathroom and held it wide open when I saw her. Sissy was flushing the toilet over and over with her head closer to the pot than I ever would have had mine. I looked over her shoulder and saw the wooden railroad ties rushing by under us as we rocked back and forth down the tracks. I wondered to myself why the toilet had not flushed onto the tracks while the train was in the station.

Even before I could close the door, Sissy lost interest in her previous activity and turned her attention to filling her sweater pockets with the tiny bars of wrapped soap from the holder on the wall. "I'm going to give these to Momma," she said with excitement in her voice.

I made her put one bar back in case another passenger needed it. Then, I suggested that she wait until we were off the train to give her gift to Momma. Of course, it couldn't be wrong to let her take the soap, since it was to be a present. After all, the railroad had put the soap out to be used by the passengers. Anyhow, I knew Momma was big on making sure us kids always did what was right and would make us put it back if we gave it to her now. If it was too late to give the soap back, I knew she would be more grateful for Sissy's efforts.

I headed back to my seat, looking out windows between each row of seats. I made a game of counting how many seats I could pass without having to grab something to steady myself against the rocking of the train. I ignored the stares of the passengers who seemed annoyed that Sissy and I had so much freedom to wander. Papa had gone up front to talk to one of the conductors in the dining car, and Momma sat lost in her thoughts, bouncing three-year-old Gertie on her lap. Momma looked so happy and peaceful, not at all how I had remembered her for most of the past couple of years. I guess she was thinking of our new start on the farm up north and a home she wouldn't have to share with any other families.

After reassuring Momma that Sissy was okay, I told her I was going up front to be with Papa. She nodded her approval. So, I resumed my game of trying to walk in a straight line as the car swayed back and forth. I zigzagged to the end of the car and kicked the brass plate at the bottom of the door. Pressure on the plate caused something to hiss and the door to open. It was neat to be able to kick a door to open it. Kicking open doors was something I wasn't allowed to do anywhere else. Standing on the platform between the cars as the door closed behind me, I could hear the wind rush by. I reached for the door to the next car... But decided not to open it.

A cool breeze was coming from an open window on the door where we had boarded the train earlier. I shook the door to make sure it was fastened. Since there was no one to tell me I couldn't look out, I stuck my head through the open window to take in the view. The wind blew my hair back as I turned to look towards the front of the train. It also slightly took my breath away. I watched with wonder as we hurried past farms where horses were working in the fields. Once in a while I got to see a tractor with dark black smoke pouring out of its tall smoke stack. The metal tires tore through the fields. For a time, I just took in the view while holding my hand and arm out the open train window and playing a game with the wind.

Near Joliet, the train slowed down a bit. That's where I saw small shacks made of wood, pieces of tin, and tar paper. They were built next to wooded areas near the railroad. Grown men sat around fires by the shacks. The train slowed enough that I could see a strange, empty look on their faces. The expression I saw was the same look of worry and hopelessness I had seen on Papa's face too many times until just a few days ago. Life had been hard after Papa let his brother have the farm up north only to then lose his own business. Now life had changed and my uncle was giving the farm back. When Papa decided to take it, that long face seemed to vanish. What I saw in those men's faces made me think about the series of events that had led up to our leaving Grandma and Grandpa, my Uncle Alex, Aunt Anna, their baby Mary Elizabeth, Mr. Brooms, and the town I grew up in.

Back at my seat, I stood on my toes to take my coat from the overhead rack and used it as a blanket to cover up Sissy, who was back in her seat. Momma nodded her head in approval and closed her own eyes contentedly. I sat down, adjusted the footrest, and again looked out the window. I didn't see much before the rocking of the train and the clickety-clack of the rails lulled me to sleep. As I drifted off, I thought back to how it had begun with spilled bathwater and a mysterious knock at the door.

CHAPTER 1

A KNOCK AT THE DOOR

It was time for our eight o'clock Saturday night baths. On other nights of the week, we could wash up at the sink, taking what Momma called a sponge bath. But on Saturdays, we each had to take our turn in the old tin washtub. Our apartment had a bathtub, but the drain leaked so taking baths to get ready for Sunday church was a complicated event. Momma had already filled the tub half-way up for Sissy and had helped her wash the hard to reach spots. It was about time for her to get out and for me to climb in.

"Momma," I heard Sissy whine, "You're not going to put Gertie in here!" I could hear Gertie padding around the outside of the tub in her bare feet and splashing the water with her hands.

Gertie liked the water. For someone her size, the old tub was like a swimming pool. She slapped the water again and in a tickled voice screamed, "Baff!" Gertie was excited and wanted to climb in with her big sister.

Sissy's voice got more desperate, "Momma, NO! I don't want her in here with me!" Gertie had slipped partway out of her diaper and was trying to lift one foot over the top lip of the metal tub. Sissy's protests grew stronger. "Momma!"

"Melissa Jean Polonec," Momma sounded back from the kitchen. "Don't raise your voice at me!" The only time Momma called my sister by her real name was when she was about to lower the boom. If Momma used our first, middle and last name, we were about to be in trouble.

I listened from the bedroom as Sissy got into trouble, figuring she deserved the scolding. Then, my mind changed as I heard Sissy continue, "Momma, Gertie will tinkle in the bathwater. I'm not going to have her in the tub with me."

That was when I remembered that *I was next* to share the water. As Momma headed towards the bathroom, I came to Sissy's defense and walked into the kitchen. "I can put Gertie in the little tub. Momma, the water in the big one is too deep for her, and she might drown."

Momma frowned at my poor attempt to avoid having to take a bath in polluted water. But without commenting, she took one of the two pots of hot water off the stove. The only hot water we had came from pots that Momma heated on the gas range. She poured the hot water into the little bitty tub she had already placed on the floor of the kitchen along with a bucket of cold water. She walked in and shooed Sissy out of the washtub. At the same time, Momma scooped Gertie into her arms and took her to the kitchen to put her in the little tub. I guess that was what she had in mind the entire time.

Sissy came out of the bathroom with a large white towel wrapped around her. She took her place at the kitchen table to wait for Momma to finish Gertie's bath and comb out her long brown hair. I took the second pan of hot water off the stove and warmed up the bathwater before climbing in.

It was while I was climbing out of the tub and toweling myself dry that trouble started. Sissy accidentally dumped over the small washtub while trying to help Gertie get out of the water. It only had about two gallons left in it. Momma had already started to empty it out using a small cooking pan and dumping it down the kitchen sink. The spill disappeared quickly between the cracks of the floor and soaked through to the ceiling below. No one had time to clean it up. Sissy sat back down in the painted white chair, still wrapped in the towel and looked at Momma to see if she was in trouble.

Momma had only one thing to say. "I hope the water didn't stain the ceiling or ruin something downstairs. If it did, Mr. Brovotsky will be up with his broom to get us all."

No sooner than Momma had spoken, we heard a loud knock at the door. We all looked as Papa walked towards the heavy six-paneled oak door that guarded our apartment. Sissy held Momma's skirt and peeked around from behind her. I moved right up by Papa and stood there like a man beside him, the two men of the family waiting to see who could be calling at this time of the night. I just hoped it wasn't Mr. Brooms again, though I didn't know why he would be at the door this late. He usually went right home after he closed up downstairs, punctually at 6:00 P.M.

Mr. Brooms was really Mr. Brovotsky, the large Polish grocer landlord. His small grocery store was on the street level of the building. Our apartment was directly above his store in downtown Coalton, Illinois. The inexpensive apartment we rented was like most of the other apartments on the top floors of the many brown brick buildings that lined the downtown area. It was a small two-bedroom flat, small but comfortable if you didn't pack five people in it, as we did.

Like most of the renters, we paid our $5 monthly rent to the owner of the store below us. I guess most landlords are not well-liked people, but our landlord, Mr. Brooms, was an especially sour-faced and sour-acting old man. I can't count the number of times that Mr. Brovotsky had beaten on the ceiling of the store with the handle of his broom when Gertie was crying. All of his pounding on the floor made such a racket that little Gertie cried even louder. After all, she had only been three months old when we lost our home on the outskirts of Coalton and moved into the apartment. During the first few weeks we lived here, Mr. Brovotsky pounded so much on the ceiling that Sissy and I started calling him Mr. Brooms when he wasn't around to hear us.

Now, even though the knock at the door came when the store was closed we were still afraid it might be Mr. Brooms. There was always the chance that he'd forgotten something or that he had paperwork to do or had some other reason to be lurking downstairs.

Momma's mention of Mr. Brooms put terror into all three of us kids. Though Gertie was too young still to know why she was afraid, she climbed into Momma's arms.

Her hand-me-down nightgown draped over Momma's strong arms. Sissy hugged Momma's skirt even tighter with one hand as she twisted a lock of her shoulder-length hair around the fingers of the other hand. She shivered as Papa slowly opened the door. I stood by Papa, expecting to see Mr. Brovotsky in his long white apron waving his broom at us and staring with his large dark eyes that were sunk back deep into his face.

Instead of Mr. Brooms, it was another familiar face, Uncle Alex. My terror quickly disappeared, and I started thinking of fun. Uncle Alex always had a good story to tell. During past visits, he had told tales about Papa growing up on the family farm in Wisconsin. Sissy's frown became a smile that spread from ear to ear as she stepped out from behind Momma. Gertie sensed the change in the air and wiggled down out of Momma's arms. She walked right over to Uncle Alex, pointed her pudgy fingers into the air and said, "Up!" That was one of the few words that she used regularly, though she jabbered constantly when you wanted her to be quiet.

I hadn't seen Uncle Alex for almost a year. At Papa's suggestion, Grandpa and Grandma had turned their farm in Wisconsin over to Uncle Alex when their tenant farmer moved out. They had been renting out the farm since moving back to Illinois, into their white two-story home by the river bottoms in Coalton. After he first took over the farm, Uncle Alex came to visit often, but he hadn't been able to come back to Coalton for some time.

Papa invited him in and gave him a hearty handshake. I started to wrap my arms around him for my usual hug; but then remembering my age, I extended my hand to shake his. After all, twelve-year-old boys don't go around hugging other men!

I guess Uncle Alex understood. He took my hand to pull me towards him. With one of his strong arms he gave me a squeeze, while with his other hand, he mussed my hair. "I almost forgot, Michael. You're almost too old to hug me nowadays, " he laughed as he winked at Papa.

Looking back at Momma, I waited for her to greet Uncle Alex. Instead of a smile and a greeting, I saw her glare at Papa with one eye cocked questioningly. She stood there in cold silence, looking back and forth from Papa to the clock on the dresser. The night became so quiet that every tick of the clock beat the air breaking the silence. Momma stood her ground, not willing to let herself become happy only to hear bad news.

Papa finally broke the icy silence and asked, "What in the world are you doing here, Alex? And where are Anna and the baby?" Before Alex could begin to answer, Papa's good nature got the best of him once again. "Brother, it's good to see you! You'll stay the night, of course. You can sleep in Michael's bed. He can sleep out on the couch. Gertie and Sissy won't mind the company. They share the same room as Michael," Papa added.

Sissy stuck her tongue out at me until a quick glance at Momma's face let her know that she'd been caught, tried, and found guilty. Her tongue pulled back inside her mouth and her cheeks flushed as she looked away from Momma's scorn. Thoughts of freedom raced through my mind. I could really escape from my two sisters for a whole night— or at least what was left of the night—and sleep on the couch.

A cough and a look from Momma put my mind back on the question of Uncle Alex's sudden appearance at our door. Uncle Alex caught her message and interrupted Papa's flow of questions. His bright eyes grew cloudy, and he looked at his feet while he began, "We've got a problem."

He paused only for a moment when Momma sternly prodded, "Well?" That one-word question demanded an answer. She stood in front of the icebox giving Uncle Alex a cold stare while waiting to find out what had happened.

"We've lost the farm! The bank's representative and the government agent came yesterday and took it away. I thought we could stall them for longer. Things just have been so bad, with the baby sick and everything."

"The baby! Where are Anna and Mary Elizabeth now?" Momma asked with a sudden change in her attitude. Despite all the outward appearance and show of hardness, we all knew Momma was soft inside—especially where babies were concerned. More than once, I'd heard her crying in Papa's arms about losing a baby when she thought none of us kids were around. She would never talk about it to any of us though. Now, when Momma heard that Alex's baby was sick, she was frantic.

"Where are Anna and the baby now?" demanded Momma again. She waved a finger in front of Uncle Alex's nose, demanding to know all the details of the whole situation.

"They're outside in the car," said Alex, nodding his head toward the open door to the outside steps. "I didn't know if we'd be welcome, he quickly added. "I thought about going to Mom's, but you know that Dad hasn't been the same since miner's consumption has gotten to his lungs. " He paused again for a moment. During the break in the talking, I thought of Grandpa recently coughing up black from all of the dirty air he had breathed into his lungs when working in the mines so many years ago.

My thoughts were broken when Uncle Alex continued, "I haven't told Dad about the farm. He thinks things are just fine with Anna and me. I'm afraid to tell him until I know how he's doing. Maybe you can go with me when I break the news. You know how he loved that farm."

⌁

Uncle Alex was talking about Grandpa, my favorite person in the entire world. Grandpa had spent much of his life working in the coal mines near Coalton, where we lived. Later, while Dad and Alex had been growing up, he and Grandma had farmed in Wisconsin. But three years ago, they came back to Coalton to live. In fact, he and Grandma had a house next to the bottoms. That's what we called the low area along the Vermillion River. Many of the mine entrances were near the river for easy loading of the coal on barges. The mines are mostly played out in that area now. But it was still a great place for me to sneak off and play when I went to Grandpa's house.

Momma again broke up my thoughts as she whirled into action. "This night air will be horrible for the baby," she scolded Alex. She quickly demanded, "Papa, put the children to bed!" She handed Gertie to Papa and gave Sissy a whack on the rear when she hesitated.

As an afterthought, she gave each a quick peck on the cheek before Papa left the room. "Not you," Momma nodded to me as I started for the bedroom to avoid getting either kissed or swatted. Neither idea appealed to me. "You come and help with Aunt Anna's things," she said as she hurried out the door.

No sooner than I had started for the door, than her voice bellowed up from halfway down the stairs, "And, Michael Andrew Polonec, put your own shoes on!" How could she even know? I walked back to the small broom closet that was just to the left of the kitchen door, that also served as our only link to the outside world. I quickly slipped off Papa's size twelve house slippers, the same old dog-eared brown slippers he usually wore every night, and put on my own shoes. I hated wearing my own shoes on Saturday night. I'd already cleaned and polished them for Sunday Mass tomorrow. Momma had always said when you go up for communion, your shoes have to be clean and shined, or the neighbors will gossip. When I realized that having to polish my shoes again would give me an excuse to stay up and listen in on the adult conversation, I felt better. I would find out what was happening! Hurrying down the steps after Momma, I raced down the alley to the car.

CHAPTER 2

LATE NIGHT VISITORS

I SKIPPED DOWN THE STEPS TWO AT A TIME, careful to avoid the squeaky step at the bottom. More than one time, that dreaded step had sounded out a warning to Mr. Brooms that I was playing on the stairs. Sometimes he was working in the back of his store and just wanted to know who was out back, but it seemed to me that he just didn't like kids. He was fine around most adults, but he always gave us kids odd looks if we were anywhere near him. Anyhow, knowing which noisy step to skip, I reached the gravel alley and turned left heading toward where I knew Momma must be by now.

It was inky black in the alley, but I could follow Momma easily by listening to her footsteps. Her strong quick footsteps could be heard ahead. I ran until I reached the back corner of the grocery. There, I stepped onto the narrow brick walkway between the store and the empty repair shop that led from the alley to Broadway out in front of the store. I could see Momma under the dimly-lit lamp post. She was standing beside Uncle Alex's 1925 Chevy, reaching for the door handle.

"Are you sure it's okay that we stay?" I heard Aunt Anna ask Momma.

Momma's answer came without a spoken word. She opened the car door with her left hand while she beckoned for Anna to hand her the baby with her right hand. Before Aunt Anna could say anything, Momma had scooped the baby up and into her arms.

Aunt Anna sat staring at Momma who still stood there in silence.

I suddenly felt the urge to say something. "What do you want me to do, Momma?" I stood ready to help—and anxious to undo the knot in the women's conversation. Aunt Anna finally got out of the car and tried to hand Momma a blanket for her daughter.

Momma smiled for the first time all night and ignored the blanket. She pulled baby Mary Elizabeth close to her and wrapped her coat around the baby to keep off the evening chill. "You help Aunt Anna carry the luggage inside. Take the long way around, son," Momma said to me, "So Aunt Anna won't trip in the alley. I'll take the baby upstairs. Papa will be right out with a light to help you." She walked quickly with Mary Elizabeth back to the alley entrance.

Aunt Anna looked confused, almost like Momma had slapped her face or something. She didn't know Momma's ways like the rest of us. Momma didn't mean to be rude. She just acted, doing what was needed when problems came up, especially when it came to family problems. Conversation wasn't as important as actions to Momma.

"What do you want me to carry up first, Aunt Anna?" I asked, trying to get her attention.

She carried the baby's things and asked me to bring up the brown leather case from the back seat. I checked to see that the car doors were locked and then led the way to the apartment. We left the black Chevy sitting under the iron lamppost and walked with our loads to the corner. Aunt Anna paused a moment as we passed by Brovotsky's

Grocery Store and came to the Ben Franklin Store on the corner. I wondered briefly if she remembered how Momma had picked out the baby's christening gown there with the money she'd been saving in the coffee can she used for a bank.

I didn't have time to ask about it. Papa was already rounding the corner with the hurricane lamp we used when it was necessary to see outside at night. We couldn't afford to buy a flashlight like some of my friends' parents had. A grin broke out on Aunt Anna's face when she saw Papa. She gave him a quick brush with her cheek against his in greeting. "Here, I'll take that," Papa said to me. As I gave the case to Papa, he handed me the lamp. I cupped my hand near the top to keep the wind out as we rounded the corner, walked to the alley, and went upstairs.

I'd forgotten to tell Aunt Anna about the squeaky step. It sang out loudly with a sour note as she stepped on it. Evidently, Mr. Brooms had gone home for the night after all. No face came to the back door of the store to give me the evil eye. Just the same, I felt better when we were all inside and the adults were all sitting at the kitchen table.

Aunt Anna took the baby from Momma and unbundled her. Meanwhile, Momma walked to the bedroom I shared with Sissy and Gertie, reaching into the stuffed closet. From the back, she pulled out Gertie's old bassinet. Gertie hadn't used it since she had started sleeping in the same bed with Sissy. Momma didn't even have to wash it off. It was always kept clean just *in case*. Momma helped Anna put the sleeping baby down for the night. Now I'd have three girls sharing my room. Yuck!

"Michael," Momma called to me, "You'd better make a bed up on the couch for tonight. Tomorrow, we'll borrow Grandma's roll-away bed. But for tonight Uncle Alex and Aunt Anna will sleep in your bed." That was the longest speech I'd heard Momma make in quite some time. Maybe it wouldn't be so bad having a baby around again, even if it did have to be a girl.

"I can't go to bed yet, Momma," I blurted out. "I got my church shoes dirty in the alley. I need to clean them up for Mass in the morning."

"Oh, let the boy stay up," said Papa. It seemed like he knew my curiosity was busting out all over about what had happened to Uncle Alex and the farm. A nod from Momma told me that it was okay.

I got Momma's scrub brush out, along with the cleaning rags and the flat can of Shinola shoe wax, preparing to spend as long as I could cleaning and polishing my shoes.

Momma took a wooden match out of the red and white tin box on the wall, turned on the gas under the front burner on the stove, and lit the pilot light. She put the old blue enamel coffee pot on the stove to boil. This was a sure sign that it was going to be a late-night with lots of conversation. She normally didn't allow Papa to brew a fresh pot of his favorite beverage this late in the evening. There wasn't enough money in Momma's hidden can of cash to waste it on more than one pot of coffee a day. Usually, if Papa wanted more coffee at night, she'd usually sprinkle only a few of the precious fresh grounds on top of the used grounds and throw a few eggshells in the water while it boiled. The eggshells were supposed to take out the bitterness.

❧

Everyone at the table sat watching the coffee pot. It wasn't until the first perk of water bubbled up the inside and started trickling through the grounds that anyone said a word. Meanwhile, I slowly spread newspapers out on the floor and sat my shoes in the middle of the front page, right on top of a picture of President Hoover. He had been elected last year and had taken office in January. I don't know who spoke first, but my attention focused on the conversation when someone used the word *Depression*. Papa and Uncle Alex agreed that the Depression was causing most of the problems faced by both families.

"I can't explain it all, "Alex started in an apologetic voice. "Everything happened at once. We had such hopes!" He looked down at the table and paused for a moment.

Aunt Anna reached over and squeezed his hand. "We're together, and that's what counts," she spoke in a supportive voice.

Momma pushed the issue. "What happened with the farm?" she asked in a firm, demanding voice.

"I was trying a new idea," said Alex, "trying to get two crops in the same year. It's too cold in Wisconsin to grow two full crops of beans or corn, but I thought I could put in an early crop of cabbage this year. The market estimates were high for early sales. Cabbage is a cool-weather crop after all," he continued. "Then I was going to plant beans to harvest in late autumn." He said all of this like the Uncle Alex I remembered. His head was held high and the sparkle in his eyes told that his dream had excited him. He paused for a moment. The enthusiasm left his voice. He looked at Papa as he went on. "You know I've always wanted to do big things."

"We all have the same thoughts," Papa responded.

"Well, big thoughts don't pay the bills or keep the bankers away from your door," said Uncle Alex bitterly. "I planted the cabbage starts too early. The weather had been so warm for the season. I jumped the gun. A heavy late frost wiped out my cabbage crop. Nearly every plant was killed or stunted. There wasn't enough left to save."

At this point, the conversation stopped. Momma stood up, not saying a word and walked over to the stove. The coffee was done. She began to pour the strong-smelling brown liquid into the heavy white china cups the adults used. While she poured, she looked over to where

I was supposed to be working. So, I poured on the steam. I started buffing my shoes with a new intensity.

Momma started to say something to me, probably to send me to bed, but Papa winked and said, "It's okay, Momma. Those shoes are filthy. It will probably take a long time tonight to get them clean enough for church in the morning." He then did something I'll always remember. He stood up and took down another heavy white cup. He reached over and poured a half of a cup of coffee in it. He added a teaspoon of sugar and filled the rest of the cup with milk from the sweating tin pitcher Momma had placed on the table. I felt ten feet tall as I put the cup of sweetened coffee—normally reserved for grown-ups —to my lips. I still didn't say anything but went back to my polishing.

I was forgotten as Aunt Anna said, "Tell them the rest, Alex." She again squeezed his hand as if she were helping the words come out of his mouth.

"Mary Elizabeth caught a cold. At least it started as a cold," Alex explained. "Then the cough and temperature got worse. We called the doctor from Phillips out to the house, but he couldn't do a lot. She seemed to keep getting sicker. We took her to the hospital at Park Falls, Wisconsin, about eighteen miles away. The cold had turned into pneumonia."

Momma interrupted, "Why didn't you call us?"

Aunt Anna answered, "It wouldn't have done any good. You would have worried, and she still wouldn't have been any better. The Doctors in Park Falls said they could help her. The hospital was willing to admit her without any cash upfront, but I felt that I needed to pay the bills right away. It seems that everyone owes the doctors so much money that the doctors are going broke."

"Using what little cash we had, I was forced to spend the seed money I'd saved for the beans. There was nothing to do but sell our two mules at auction. The bank had foreclosed on a neighbor's farm and was selling everything. They consented to sell the mules and some of our equipment for a percentage of the sale. It all went to good use," Alex laughed. We're broke as heck, but our baby is okay."

"Family is the most important thing in the world," agreed Momma with a strangely angry look on her face. "Family should come before anyone or anything else!" She directed this comment at Papa. Momma had never quite forgiven Papa for having brought her family to such a low state that we had to live above a grocery store.

As the eldest son, Papa had been given the first chance to take over the family farm in Wisconsin. Grandpa had bought it when he quit mining years ago. When he moved back to Coalton, he rented out the farm at first. When the tenant farmer moved, Grandpa offered Papa the first chance to take over the farm note at the bank. Papa knew how badly Uncle Alex wanted the farm and gave him the chance to manage it. That was Papa's first mistake in Momma's eyes. The second mistake was one that caused Momma to stop being the smiling, happy person that I knew when I was little and turned her personality into one that was like a smoking volcano. You never knew when she might erupt.

After Papa gave up the farm, he bought a small business in Coalton. That was about the time the stock market crashed and I first heard the word Depression. Papa hadn't invested in stocks, but two of his partners had. They needed money desperately to cover their losses. Against Momma's advice, Papa readily gave them back the money they'd invested in the business and assumed the debt himself. Then, the banks closed across most of the country. Papa didn't have the money to pay the bank when they called in the loan. That's when the bank took the business away. Strike two in Momma's eyes!

Strike three came a few months later. Gertie was three months old when it happened. Lots of the people that Papa owed for business supplies demanded payment. Papa sold our house so he could pay everyone back. Momma had argued that family came first! No one else was paying off debts to people who didn't have the power to force them to, so why should Papa? She wasn't uncaring, but in her view, the family had to come first!

Suddenly, Momma looked at Uncle Alex in a more friendly light. She poured everyone another cup of coffee, starting with Uncle Alex. It was odd how both he and Papa had lost their homes, but Uncle Alex had lost his to care for the baby. He took care of his family first, and that was important to Momma!

I made the mistake of clinking my spoon against the side of my empty cup and called attention to myself. "The shoes are good enough," Momma said to me. "Any more rubbing and you'll wear the leather out. Off to bed!"

I put the top on the Shinola can and put it in the rack Papa had built inside the cabinet door under the sink. I folded the dirty rags and left them on the paper along with my shoes. They would sit there until morning. Then, I laid down on the couch in the next room, covered up with the quilt that Momma brought me, and tried to listen to the adults' conversation without being too obvious about it.

"I tried to get a loan from the bank, so I could still get a crop in," Uncle Alex continued, "But, the bank manager said my ideas about farming were strange. They said if I'd put in a normal crop like a normal farmer, I wouldn't have spent my savings and I wouldn't be asking for a loan now."

He claimed if the bank loaned money to kooks like me, it would start a run on the bank like the ones that have wiped out many banks across the country already. "Maybe the people at the bank are right, but they didn't even give me a chance. I tried to stall them. I even ignored the bank representative when he first came to my door, but when he came back with the government agent and the sheriff, they had an eviction notice. I had no choice but to pack up and leave.

"At least one thing went my way, however," Uncle Alex went on. "The bank didn't have anyone to sell the farm to. No one has the extra cash needed to pay the down payment. So the bank took out a lien on the farm. Right now, they're letting a sharecropper plant beans, so they can get a crop. He paid for the seeds out of his pocket. He's doing the work, and they still get half of the profit. It doesn't seem fair," I heard him say as my eyelids started getting heavy. He said something about paying off something and something else about interest by next season. I didn't know why he would have to worry about next year if the farm was already lost.

Probably a lot more was talked about, but I don't remember any of it. All I know is that when that late-night began, we were a family of five, and as I went to sleep, we had three more people living in our apartment above Mr. Broom's Store.

CHAPTER 3

SECRET SPOT IN THE BOTTOMS

THE VERY NEXT DAY WAS SUNDAY. I woke up earlier than my sisters, yet I had to wait in line to get into the bedroom to get dressed. I loved Uncle Alex and Aunt Anna, but I could already see how my life might be different with three more people to share our already crowded apartment. I even had to wait longer to use the bathroom. Only the baby didn't have that problem. I thought about that as I started into the bedroom where Aunt Anna was changing her. Phew! I held my breath as I ran to the closet for my church shirt and pants and got out of there in a hurry so I could breathe again.

There was one thing that looked good though: with two people cooking, we were going to eat well. Sissy and I ate pancakes, eggs, and sausages. I had picked out a white china cup and put it on the table next to my plate, hoping to get the adult's beverage, coffee again, but Momma just poured it full of milk and pushed it in front of me.

Gertie stuffed her breakfast in her ears and tried to wear part of it in her hair. I hoped that she would learn to eventually put part of the food in her mouth without help. At least she was farther on her way than Mary Elizabeth, who was taking her bottle in Momma's arms.

We men left the apartment while the ladies cleaned up, visited, and got the girls ready for Mass. We headed for Grandpa's house. It was too early to pick up Grandma and Grandpa for church, but I figured Papa and Uncle Alex had their reasons for leaving early and didn't ask why. It was only a short distance across town to their house, which sat right on the little bluff overlooking the bottoms. Often, I would make the trip on foot by myself. By cutting through yards and alleys, I could make it there in less than fifteen minutes. Today, we took Uncle Alex's car. It took us about eight minutes to get there.

Just as we pulled up in front, Grandpa's dog, Pal, a short brown bulldog, waddled out of the front door. He sat down beside one of the wooden columns next to the front steps, then started snorting at us. For as long as I could remember, Pal hadn't barked, he only snorted. Pal didn't get along with just anyone. Usually, he only responded to Grandpa and me.

Grandpa said that he had gotten Pal when a railroad worker had abandoned him. Grandpa also said that, for a long time, Pal wouldn't even allow himself to be petted. For some time, he howled mournfully every time the train whistle blew. But as Pal got to know Grandpa, he followed him wherever he went… that is, until Grandpa took sick. When the coughing fits began, Grandpa got winded easily and gave up his daily walks with Pal. That's when Pal started following me. If anyone else tried to touch or pet Pal, he would snort, show his teeth, and blow snot all over their legs. So far, no one had ever tried to pet Pal a second time.

Papa and Uncle Alex went inside. I stayed out front with Pal. I reached down to wipe the drool off the sides of his mouth and to pet him. He didn't look right. It's funny, but it seems if I remember right,

Pal started slowing down about the same time that Grandpa took sick. Grandpa would cough, and Pal would snort. Grandpa would wheeze, and Pal would slobber. More and more, I had to take Pal for a drag, because he sat down and refused to walk.

Grandma popped her head out the door. "What's the matter?" she asked. "Do you love that old dog more than you do me? Get over here and give your Grandma a hug."

I started over to Grandma, and Pal waddled beside me. Part of his extra weight probably came from the snacks that Grandpa constantly fed him. I thought to myself, "Maybe that's why he's slowing down!"

I gave Grandma a hug, which was no easy thing to do, My Grandma was BIG! She preferred to use the word "stout" to describe herself, but BIG was the word that came to my mind every time she wanted a hug. *A boy could get lost and suffocate in the folds of her body,* I thought as she wrapped her strong arms around me, yet I couldn't call her fat. Her years of farm labor had given her a strength that few people have. A hug from Grandma would leave you full of love and give you an aching body.

Pal tried to get inside to be with Grandpa. He stood beside the door snorting and looking at her. "Not yet," she said to Pal, "Not until you take a walk with Michael. I won't have you making any messes around this house just because you're too lazy to walk to the bottoms." Pal snorted again and blew snot on the porch by her feet.

"Michael," she looked at me, "Take this creature down to the bottoms and walk him before I beat him. I'll be ready for Mass in a bit. Your Dad and Alex are in talking to Grandpa. I don't know what's happening yet, but I can guess that it's not good news." Now, the last thing that Momma had said to me before leaving the house was to stay out of the bottoms and to keep my clothes clean; but how can a boy argue with his Grandma?

I started walking down the steep path through the cane that led to the bottoms. As I walked with Pal waddling behind me, my face hit something sticky. I stopped right away and threw up my hands protectively. I began pulling sticky threads off my face. I looked around. A morning spider web hung across the path, still glistening with the morning dew. It sat there like a full larder, waiting for the spider to come back and collect the waiting meal of insects that had chanced to land upon it during the night. I ran into one of the strings of webbing that held the huge trap across the path. It didn't seem right to tear it down, so I walked off the path around it. Pal wasn't about to waste any energy and plowed right through the bottom of the web. It was comical to watch him afterwards. He would waddle a few feet, then snort and try to lick the webbing off his face. All he accomplished was to spread drool all over his face. So, I stopped and helped Pal to clean off the web.

Pal licked my face while I was bent over, to say thanks. Then, he finished waddling down the path to a point where the ravine leveled out and went straight towards his tree. It was always the same. Pal had to sniff his tree first, to see if any other dogs had been around. He would do the same with every tree in about a thirty foot radius before coming back to his own tree to do what Grandma had sent us down here for.

I knew that I had about a five minute wait, so while Pal sniffed around by his trees, I checked my secret spot. No one else, except for Grandpa, even knew I had a secret spot. Although I hinted at where it was, I didn't tell him all about it. I told Grandpa about this place that I called my fort. It was only a few feet off the path by Pal's tree, hidden from view by several gooseberry bushes. I don't know what Grandpa thought it was, probably just a wooden box with a door in it or just a hole dug into the hillside like lots of other kids had done. But my spot was better. I had found a vent hole from one of the deserted old coal mines. The opening that had connected the vent hole to the old mine had been closed tight. Little by little, I had dug an opening of my own. One of my goals was to get into the old mine to do some exploring.

I was really careful as I moved aside the brush that stood in front of the hole. I wouldn't be able to face Momma if I tore my only suit coat on the tiny stickers that poked out from the small branches. Right outside the opening, I kept a long forked stick. Before entering, I poked the stick inside and moved it back and forth as far as my arm would reach. I listened carefully for any rattling sounds. Hearing none, I knew it was safe to go inside. I stepped through the opening and felt along the wall for my match tin. After striking the tip on the front of my zipper, I held up the wooden match out in front of me and looked around. Everything was just as I had left it earlier in the week.

Knowing that I had better be getting back to the house, I started to turn around … when the match blew out. That's when I heard an ominous rattling noise. Fear ran through my entire body. I was afraid to reach for my matches for fear of touching something else. I sat totally still and the rattling stopped. I cautiously began to work my way back to the opening. Then the rattling came back even louder. Panicked, I threw myself out of the opening and into the sunlight, grabbing my stick and whipping around, ready for action.

Just as I reached out with the stick, "Snort!" Pal blew snot at my ankles. He was angry that I had left him. He had rattled his way past the gooseberry bush to the opening of my secret spot. Now, he and Grandpa knew where it was located. As my heart stopped beating too fast, I took a moment to wipe some of the clay and Pal's drools off my clothes. As I cleaned up, I reminded myself to bring some candles and a knife when I came back to my secret spot again.

Back we went, heading for the house at the top of the bottoms. Pal sat down on the way several times, demanding to be carried. NO

WAY! I wasn't going to get more mud *plus* dog hair all over my suit. I'd never hear the end of it from Momma.

Back at the house, Grandpa had decided to stay home from church. The news about the farm had upset him, and he wanted to be alone with his pipe and his thoughts. Before we left, however, he called, "Mikie, Come in here. Let me get a look at you!" As Pal and I entered the room, Pal showed the first bit of energy that I'd seen from him all day. He jumped right up on the hassock, or footstool, where Grandpa's huge feet rested with one toe sticking out of his sock.

Pal did something then that I truly didn't understand. He laid his face right down on Grandpa's feet and went to sleep. "Grandpa said, "With all Pal's slobbers washing my feet, I won't have to wash them this week. I hoped he was kidding, but I couldn't be sure!

Grandpa and I had visited for just a few minutes when he said, "Your Pa said you were quite a grown-up last night, drinking coffee, polishing your shoes, and not asking questions!"

At the mention of my shoes, I looked down at the floor. My walk through the clay and mud in the bottoms had gotten them filthy again. Grandpa picked up on my worried look and got up to help me quickly put things in order again. Trust a Grandpa to help in emergencies. He had me spotless and my shoes shining brightly by the time that Grandma came in.

"I'm ready for Mass," she said. "And, what's this old goat doing up off his rocker? I thought you were too sick to go to Mass with us," she said to Grandpa.

Grandpa just winked at me and coughed. When he did that, Pal snorted and blew snot at Grandma again.

"Well, I never!" she exclaimed. "Come on, Michael," she said to me. We'll leave those two at home. And they're the ones who need to go to Mass, that old man and his dog!" Although she sounded angry,

I knew she loved Grandpa. Pal, however, was another story. Grandpa ignored her, crossing his legs on the footstool and lighting up his pipe once more as we walked out the door together.

Uncle Alex and Dad sat up front, while Grandma and I sat in the back. We pulled up to the back of the alley at the apartment just as the girls came out. Sissy came down the steps first with Aunt Anna brushing her hair as she walked. She was walking proudly in what looked like a new skirt. When I looked twice, however, I saw that either Momma or Aunt Anna had fastened a new bow and some lace on the front of Sissy's old Sunday dress. It made me feel good inside to see my sister so happy. Best of all, Momma was smiling too. She walked down the steps behind Aunt Anna with Gertie on one hip and the baby held comfortably in her other arm.

Squeak, Squeak, Squeak! Our noisy, tell-tale step played tattle-tale as each family member stepped on it. No one seemed to notice except me. They all piled into the car to head for St. Edwards.

CHAPTER 4

MESSY MASS AT SAINT EDWARDS

Sissy climbed into the car between Papa and Uncle Alex, while Momma, Aunt Anna, and the two little ones squeezed into the back with Grandma. I commented that there wasn't room for me in the car. Before Momma could protest, I shut the back door and jumped onto the running board. I stood on the eight-inch-wide platform that ran alongside the bottom edge between the front and rear tires on the passenger side of the car, filled with joy as Uncle Alex drove out of the alley taking us all to Mass at Saint Edwards.

Away we went to church. Uncle Alex drove the side streets, so I wouldn't fall off in traffic. I gripped the inside of the door with my right hand while holding the back of the seat behind Momma with my left. Momma didn't approve of me standing on the running board as the car drove down the street and voiced her opinion as she grabbed my wrist. I complained that I wasn't a baby, but secretly I was glad she had ahold of me. We were going nearly twenty miles an hour. At one point, Uncle Alex came a little too close to the curb and my pant cuff brushed against a trash can that had been left out by the street as we drove by it. That's when I made Momma feel better by promising to ride on someone's lap inside or to walk on the way home.

My tie kept slapping me in the face. Gertie got a charge out of it and started giggling. I would have liked to take the tie off, but I couldn't. You weren't considered religious by Momma if you didn't have a properly tied tie and clean, shiny shoes when you went to Mass on Sundays. I had to remember to thank Grandpa for helping me clean my shoes off after my visit to the bottoms. Now, there was no evidence to convict me. She'd only know I had been in the bottoms if my shoes were muddy.

Uncle Alex held out his left arm, bent with his hand and fingers pointing toward the sky to signal a right turn. The car slowed for a moment. I took this opportunity to pull my hand out of Momma's tight grip. I waved at my school friends as we drove by them and turned into the parking lot. It was the cat's meow to be seen riding on the running board. Everyone would envy me. Of course they would have laughed if they'd seen Momma holding my hand. I turned around while stepping down off the running board to see if they had noticed me.

That's when it happened! I stepped right into what must have been the biggest mud puddle in town. The mud oozed up over the tops of my shoes as the sucking action of the mud tried to pull me deeper.

I knew I was in trouble and had to take action fast. I quickly darted around the car and opened the back door on the opposite side for Aunt Anna and the others. I told Momma that I'd run inside in case one of the altar boys hadn't shown up. I knew that it wasn't my turn to help with Mass as a server—and that Father Zarecki always had a back-up server just in case an altar boy was ill—But Momma didn't know it!

It was obvious to me as I squished across the parking lot that my elegant gesture to help the priest impressed Momma and Grandma. In Momma's mind, I was probably storing up points with God in heaven. However, in my mind, I planned to run into the church before Momma could see my feet and start quizzing me about going to the bottoms. I couldn't lie to Momma, but it's not lying if Momma doesn't ask. If she wasn't going to ask about the bottoms, I wasn't going to tell her.

I ran to the side door of the church that led down a hall to the vestibule where the priest and the altar boys got dressed. My plan was to hurry past them all and head straight for the bathroom where I could clean up.

"The Lord be praised," said Father Zarecki, and his large hand landed on my shoulder. "I was outside in front of the church looking for someone to help with Mass. We have a really full church today, and I need extra help. Just as I'd given up hope, here came your Mother. I haven't seen her smile like that in quite a while, Michael. She was really impressed that you had been in such a hurry to help me. The Lord will bless you for your efforts on his behalf. Hurry and get dressed. God will give you the reward that you deserve."

Why did he have to say that? That wasn't what I wanted to hear. My feet were soaked. My shoes were muddy! God knew that I had been in the bottoms and He was getting His revenge!

Not one to give up easily, I ran into the vestibule and grabbed the longest cassock I could find. No one could see my feet if my robe was long enough, and surely no one would fault a last minute addition to the line of altar boys for not having time to find a robe the right size. Robe in place! Out the door! Into line! Yes, luck was with me. No one would need to know.

Oh, no, the noise! A hiss sounded every time I took a step, as the water squeezed out of my shoes. I looked up in alarm at the cross at the front of the church and said a silent prayer. Then, the off-key organ player started in. She wasn't good, but she was loud, and at that moment, her playing sounded lovely to me.

I folded my hands and said a silent thank you. I put a holy look on my face as I started walking up the main aisle. Grandma and the others were all kneeling in prayer. I walked right by Momma. She didn't even notice as she sat on the hard pew holding Mary Elizabeth. She wasn't even looking my way. A few more seconds and I would have been home free. I would have committed the perfect crime right inside of God's house.

The only eyes on me belonged to my sister, Gertie. She looked so angelic, sitting beside Momma, but Momma's constant doting on the baby was beginning to annoy her. Then Gertie saw the perfect person to give her some attention. That person was me!

Before anyone could stop her, Gertie scooted right past Momma and she ran up the aisle behind me. She pulled at my cassock and said her favorite word, "UP!" Her pudgy little fingers pointed into the air. I looked down at her. I wanted to laugh, but when I saw the trail of wet muddy prints that I'd left, I no longer wanted to laugh.

I looked at Father Zarecki, but he was already reading from the Old Testament at the pulpit. At least he hadn't seen. I looked at Momma, hoping she wouldn't look down.

Momma handed Mary Elizabeth back to Aunt Anna and walked quickly to pick up Gertie. I wish she hadn't been quite so embarrassed. Her eyes were on the floor all the way to the front of the church. But they weren't focused on Gertie. Instead, her eyes were on a set of mysterious muddy foot prints that led all the way back down the aisle.

It didn't seem fair! Momma didn't even look at the other boys. Why, any one of them could have done it! No, she looked right at me. She picked up Gertie and backed up all the way to her seat.

Father Zarecki was leading the congregation in the Lord's Prayer, but Momma's lips weren't saying a prayer. They were mouthing the words, "Michael Andrew Polonec!" I was in trouble. Mothers never use your full Christian name unless you're in trouble.

I don't remember what was said in the sermon. I spent the whole time silently praying that Momma would hear any words the priest said about forgiveness.

I guess it could have been a lot worse! After Mass, Momma asked how I'd gotten my feet dirty. I told her the truth. The mud on my feet hadn't come from the bottoms, but from the church parking lot. Father Zarecki looked at me and smiled. He sensed that I had more to tell. I always thought that confession was supposed to be private between a sinner and the priest. I mean it's not so bad clearing your conscience by telling the priest what you've done wrong. But, holy cow! To have to tell your Mother! That hurt!

My punishment was to spend the entire afternoon cleaning all of the carpets at St. Edwards. I tried pleading that Sunday was supposed to be a day of rest, but Momma insisted that I clean the carpet before the five o'clock Mass. I couldn't believe my rotten luck. I'd planned to spend part of the day searching through the junkyard looking for a candle to take to my secret place.

I did feel better, however, when Father Zarecki complimented the good job I was doing on the carpet. I liked our priest. He was a pretty special person. He had married my parents years ago. When I came along, I was named after Father Michael Zarecki. My two sisters and I had all been baptized by him as well. He looked after our whole family in life and ... I was daydreaming when Father Zarecki came up behind me.

"I have one more job for you, Michael," he said. I just rolled my eyeballs, thinking the worst. "Take this can," Father Zarecki continued. He handed me a large empty three pound coffee can. I didn't know that priests drank so much coffee. "Michael," he continued. "Take this can and scrape the wax out of all of the prayer candles. New ones have been donated to the church, and I want to get rid of all of the old wax."

The perfect way to get rid of it popped into my mind. All of that wax could be melted together to make one giant candle for my secret place. I guess the Lord *does* listen to the prayers of young boys, even ones who make a mess at Mass.

CHAPTER 5

AFTER-SCHOOL WALKS

SEVERAL WEEKS HAD PASSED SINCE THE INCIDENT AT ST. EDWARDS. The apartment seemed more crowded than it had the first few days. The newness of having a bigger family was wearing off. There wasn't a lot of room around the place, and I needed some time alone. Momma always made certain to keep me too busy to visit the bottoms. Even my trips to Grandpa's were monitored. Momma insisted that I took Sissy with me everywhere. Sissy was under orders by Momma to report any trips I made anywhere near the river bottoms. It didn't seem fair!

Every day we stopped by Grandpa's on the way home from school to visit and to walk Pal. We'd always see Grandpa out on the front porch sitting in his rocker in front of the open living room window. He'd be sitting with his pipe clenched in his teeth, waiting for us to arrive. The only time he left his chair outside was to change chairs. He sat inside when the weather turned cold.

Our after school visits were nearly the same every day. Grandma would usually have lemonade for us. After we cooled off, she would take Sissy aside to teach her a new crochet stitch or to show her off her quilting. Grandma was really big on girls learning how to do "women's work," whether Sissy wanted to learn it or not. For Grandma, however, this meant doing almost all of the work. Grandpa had hardly been moving around, or doing as much as he usually had in the past.

While the two females worked, Grandpa and I would visit about the problems of the world. He was really upset about the farm and about Uncle Alex being out of work. I wished I could do something about either of those problems.

After we talked for a bit, Grandpa would doze off. That's when I would walk Pal. Lately, the walks had been short trips around the neighborhood. I walked Pal up and down the red brick streets. I was worried that Sissy would tell if I went down to the bottoms. I hoped I'd find an excuse to get away. I had brought the candle wax and some candle wicking home, stashing it under the porch the day after the mess at St. Edwards. But I had yet to make my new candle out of it.

My visit on that day started as usual. Grandpa was there as always, sitting patiently. Pal was the impatient one. As we walked up that day, Pal snorted at me and gave me a look like I should have been there the entire time instead of going to school. Of course, that would have been fine with me. But even easy going Papa wouldn't allow that.

Grandma brought out the lemonade like she ordinarily did, but this time she also carried a plate with several cookies on it. "Thank you, Grandma," Sissy and I said nearly at the same time.

"Snort!" said Pal. Then, the gray stiff-haired pooch looked up at Grandma as if to say, "Where's mine?"

"You're too fat!" Grandma told Pal. "You're not getting a cookie." Then, she scooted him out of her way with her foot.

Pal got up and waddled over in front of her. "SNORT!" went Pal again!

"Grandma said, NO C-O-O-K-I-E!" I couldn't believe it. She spelled out "cookie" for the dog! The craziest thing was that he sat there looking angry as if he understood her! That's when it happened. Pal walked up and blew snot all over her feet and walked away. I'd swear I heard that dog laugh under his breath as he walked away.

"That's it, old man!" Grandma screamed at Grandpa. "I'm going to get rid of you and that dog!

Grandpa just sat there taking it all in. He'd heard it all before. In fact, he often heard parts of this message more than once a day. Sissy and I sat there and laughed at Grandma's ravings.

"You think I don't mean it?" She directed her comments at us. "Well, I'm serious." When that old man dies, I'm throwing that dog out of here!" She then walked out and wiped her shoes on the grass.

The smell of grass reminded me that sometime soon I'd get to mow the lawn for Grandpa. I loved the smell of the freshly cut grass that fell out behind the whirling blades of the push mower. Grandpa had promised to teach me how to sharpen the blades before I mowed again. I just had to catch him on a day when he had more energy. Grandpa seemed to be getting more tired every day.

"That dog!" started Grandma again. She'd stepped on a "present" that Pal had left in the grass and turned back to Grandpa and me again. No more of these short walks! Starting next Monday, I want you to take Pal down to the bottoms *every day*. He needs a longer walk, and my grass needs a rest! I'll clear it with your Mother.

I walked home a happy boy. I loved that house at the top of the bottoms.

CHAPTER 6

LEARNING ABOUT MR. BROOMS

THE NEXT DAY WAS SATURDAY. It was supposed to be a day of fun for me. Instead, it became another day of spending time with my sister. As sister's go, Sissy wasn't too bad, but enough was enough. I wanted some time alone. But Papa was at work at the tile factory again. Uncle Alex spent his days walking from store to store looking for work. That's where he was that morning. Momma and Aunt Anna had to care for the babies and do the housework, so my job was to provide entertainment for my sister.

Sissy and I had been sent downstairs by Momma to talk to Mr. Brooms about buying his old fruits and vegetables. She often bought the food he was about to toss out, and she got the food at a large discount, especially since we had more mouths to feed. We didn't mind, though. She cut out the bad spots from the fruit and made some delicious fruit salads. The drooping vegetables seemed to perk up when she soaked them in cold water, made cool with the chunks of ice purchased from the iceman on his way back home from his deliveries. Even the garbage had a use. We hauled it over to Grandma's and fed it to her hogs.

The only bad part about getting the old food was dealing with Mr. Brooms. This was one place where I didn't mind having Sissy along. Mr. Brooms seemed to tolerate girls much better than he did boys! He talked to Sissy. He snapped at me!

That's how Sissy ended up being the one to sweet talk Mr. Brooms into giving us a lower than usual price for the old fruits and vegetables. I had made plans with my friends to go to the movies. A new film, *All Quiet on the Western Front,* was playing. I didn't have the ten cents it would take to go and had been trying to think of a way to get Momma to part with a dime. Then I had a thought, it might be easier to get two dimes out of Momma than to get one!

I might be able to get Momma to pay for the movies if I could first show her where we had saved more than the twenty cents on the family's grocery bill. I'd have to work on getting her to look at me as the generous older brother taking his little sister to the movies. But I couldn't let her know what was playing or who else was going. It was all in how things were presented.

I sent Sissy back to talk to Mr. Brooms while I looked over the fruit and vegetable section. The first thing I saw was an ugly brown piece of flypaper hanging over the stack of crates. Usually, the sticky tape waved around in the breeze. But the air that usually blew across the open front of the store was still right now. As I looked at the tape, it hung heavily, loaded with dead flies. The odors of the ripe melons were more pungent than usual. This could be bad news for Mr. Brooms. I wondered how I could use this knowledge to my advantage.

I walked up in time to hear Sissy tell Mr. Brooms how clean he kept his store. He stood in his long white apron leaning on the long handle of his straw-bristled broom. The broom had a dust rag wrapped around it. Apparently, he had been knocking the cobwebs out of the corners.

The smile on his face disappeared when I walked up. I didn't understand it! I had never done anything bad around him or said anything rude. He turned his back on me as I walked up. He took the dust rag off the bristles and started sweeping the wooden floor.

"Hey, Mr. Brovotsky," I called out to his back. "What's with all of the flies?"

He whipped around and glared at me. "There are no flies in my store," he stated firmly in a hoarse voice.

"But what about the flies hanging over the fruit?" I asked. Mr. Brooms strode to the front of the store. I followed in his footsteps. When he reached the fruit crates, he reached upward with the handle of his broom towards the ceiling that also served as our apartment floor. He hit the nail that held the flypaper in place three times. I heard Gertie start crying upstairs and the footsteps of either Momma or Aunt Anna walking to pick her up. On the fourth attempt, he dislodged the flypaper and caught the wooden spool that weighted it down.

Two things caught my attention. First, he had hit the ceiling with his broom to do his work, not to be mean to anyone upstairs. Second, I was amazed by how fast his hand had shot out to grab the falling tape and keep it out of the groceries. I'd never thought of Mr. Broom's being fast at anything.

"I think," I started, "that something is causing your fruit to rot, and its drawing flies." I was proud of my observation.

"What you think doesn't matter," he replied curtly. "I've got a broken fan, so no air is blowing to keep the front of the store cool." I'd already figured that out, but I didn't tell him that. I followed him over to a large red barrel with a lid on it where he kept the garbage.

"You're not going to be able to sell all of that fruit, Mr. Brovotsky," Sissy hinted in a concerned voice. "No one is going to want stuff that smells and has flies on it." Mr. Broom's attention turned from the seriousness of his problem to smile as my sister talked to him. My sister did have a way with people.

"Yeah," I said, trying to come out ahead in this exchange.

"Garbage!" he muttered grumpily to me. He picked up one of the crates and started to a back room in the store where a door led out to the alley. I wasn't invited to follow him, but he didn't tell me I couldn't come into the back. I'd only seen this part of the store from the stairs that led up to our apartment. That was when the door was open. I stood by a cluttered desk near that door while Mr. Brovotsky set the crate down. I picked up a picture that sat on the desk. It was a photo of a man in uniform who looked a lot like Mr. Brooms.

"Is this you?" I asked without thinking. A hand shot out and grabbed the picture out of my hands.

"No one told you to come back here," said Mr. Brooms. He had a different look on his face than any I had ever seen before. I didn't know if he was going to hit me or to cry, and I don't think he knew either. He just stood there looking at the picture. "You boys are all alike. You don't care for anyone but yourself."

"Is that your son, Mr. Brovotsky?" asked a little voice behind the white-haired man. "I think he's handsome just like you." Sissy stood looking up at Mr. Brooms. A tear squeezed itself out of the corner of one of his eyes.

"He would have been twenty nine years o ..." he caught himself and stopped. "Michael Polonec, Get out of here! I've got a store to run and a fan to fix."

I left right away and took Sissy with me. We walked out the front of the store and around the corner to get back to the alley. Sissy kept trying to ask me questions. I thought I knew some of the answers, but I hadn't sorted them all out yet. So I didn't answer. When we reached the stairs to the apartment, Sissy started straight up while I just stared at the back door of the store.

"Squeak!" Sissy stepped on the bad step. The door to the store opened. I expected to receive a mean look from Mr. Brooms because we'd bothered him so much. But instead, his eyes met mine and we just stared at each other for a moment. He still had the picture in one hand. He had a large red handkerchief in the other hand. He wiped his eyes and walked slowly back into the store, closing the door behind him.

We didn't have Momma's fruits and vegetables, and I hadn't gotten my dimes for the movies. But I had gotten to know our landlord a little better. I knew that I would never look at Mr. Brooms quite the same again.

CHAPTER 7

HELPING HANDS AND BROKEN FANS

"Why isn't Mr. Brooms married," Sissy was asking Momma as I reached the top of the stairs. I didn't know if Momma would respond or not, so I sat down on the top of the porch railing and stayed outside the screen door to listen. I peeled at the loose paint on the rail while I waited to hear what Momma said.

"He was," Momma answered briefly. She got up from the table and tossed the potato peelings into the trash can. Then, she sat down to snap the green beans. "His wife died before Michael was born." Momma placed part of the beans in front of Sissy who automatically started to help her. She snapped the ends off the beans and broke the beans into bite-size pieces—Grandma's training was taking over.

Sissy followed up, "Did he have a son?"

Momma was silent for a long time while she continued to snap beans, so I got up and peeked in through the copper screen on the door. Momma had one of those "I'm not so sure you need to know this" looks on her face. I gritted my teeth and silently willed her to answer.

"Why?" Momma inquired. I was getting tired of short answers. I wanted to find out about Mr. Brooms even more than Sissy did! A crunching sound was coming down the alley, and I recognized the sound of Uncle Alex's footsteps. If he came in with more bad news of not being able to find a job, I'd never find out about Mr. Brooms' son.

"Michael was helping Mr. Brooms with his fruit and stuff," Sissy began, "and we saw a picture of a soldier. The picture looked just like Mr. Brooms."

Please hurry! I thought to myself. Uncle Alex had reached the bottom of the stairs. Luckily, he put one foot on the bottom step and bent over to tie his shoelace.

Momma must have been reading my mind. "Mr. Brovotsky's son left to fight in the Great War in 1917. He was killed in France right before the end of the war. Mr. Brovotsky hasn't been the same since. But he's a good man. You and Michael stay out of his way."

Just in time! I had the answers to my questions. Uncle Alex reached the top step and opened the door. "Michael," he said as he looked my way. I thought he was going to tell me to stay off the porch railing. "Where did your Dad put his tools?"

"What are you going to fix?" I asked. My interest perked up. I'd learned a few days ago that Uncle Alex was quite handy around the house. He'd fixed our tub and water heater, so we didn't have to take our baths in the kitchen anymore.

My uncle closed the door long enough to talk to me. "The car's been overheating, so I'm going to try to fix the fan on the engine," he said.

The word "fan" triggered a solution to Mr. Brooms' problem in my mind. "Can you come to the store with me?" I asked.

"I might be able to," he replied. "What are you up to now?"

I didn't want to tell him, so I said, "It's kind of a nice surprise for Mr. Brooms."

He gave me a quizzical look, then decided to humor me. "Let me tell Anna that I'm home. I promised to take Mary Elizabeth out for a bit."

I thought this was kind of weird. No other dads I knew spent so much time caring for their babies. Most let the moms do all of the work. Uncle Alex was different, but I kind of wished that Papa had that kind of time to spend with me. But by the time he came home after working ten hours at the tile factory on the other side of the bottoms, he was too tired to move. Besides the long day, he walked to and from work in order to save money. The price of gas was now up to seventeen cents a gallon.

While Uncle Alex visited with the ladies, I told Momma that I was going back downstairs. I said that Mr. Brooms needed me to help him. She looked at me in disbelief, but she didn't say anything. It wasn't like I was lying. He did need me. He just didn't know it yet.

I had found that I could go more places if I told Momma where I was going and left quickly. It was too easy for her to say "NO!" if I asked for permission. After I gave her the few seconds that politeness called for to disagree, I grabbed Papa's toolbox and went back outside to wait in the sunshine on the porch.

A few minutes later, Uncle Alex came out carrying Mary Elizabeth in his right arm. He had a big smile on his face and held her with pride. "Let's go, mystery boy," he said to me. He started down the stairs, carefully holding the rail with his left hand.

We talked as we took the long way around the block to the front of the grocery store. I told Uncle Alex what I'd learned about Mr. Brovotsky and commented that he had no one to help him out around the store. Uncle Alex said that most of the stores around town were short of help. But no one could take the chance to hire extra help with the Depression going on.

By that time, we'd reached the front of the store. Uncle Alex stopped long enough to toss Mary Elizabeth into the air several times and hear her giggle. While they played, I went into the store to talk to Mr. Brooms.

"What do you want?" he demanded when he saw me. "Did you come back to tease an old man again and tell him how many flies he has in his store? Why don't you go bother someone else?" His words hurt my feelings, but I understood now that maybe he didn't mean to act so rudely. I thought he might even be lonely.

"We've come to fix your fan," I said, without backing away from him as I usually did.

"Who's *we*," he asked as he looked around. "You and your little sister?"

"No, Sir. Me and my Uncle Alex, Sir. He can fix almost anything." Hearing me mention his name, my Uncle walked into view. Mr. Brooms looked doubtfully at my Uncle. I could almost read his mind. *How could a man who carried around a baby fix anything with a kid in his arms?*

"Where's this broken fan?" inquired my Uncle.

"Right over here," said Mr. Brooms. He pointed to the broken fixture that hung down over the cracker barrel pointing towards the discolored fruits and vegetables.

Before Mr. Brooms could protest, Uncle Alex said, "Here! Take her." He handed Mary Elizabeth to the shocked store owner. Mr. Brooms stood there with his mouth open, while Uncle Alex put the lid on the cracker barrel and climbed on top of it. "Hand me the screwdriver," he commanded as he went to work replacing two frayed wires in the back.

I quickly did as he asked, the whole time watching to see what Mr. Brooms did with the baby. I almost doubled over in laughter as

Mary Elizabeth took a finger out of her drooling mouth and stuck it up Mr. Brooms' nose. I thought he might throw her on the floor or do something worse, but he just laughed and gave her a hug. Maybe I was right. He was just lonely. People need to have other people around them.

We worked until the fan was blowing once again. With air circulating, the temperature in the store seemed to drop quickly. As we put the tools into the box, Uncle Alex held out his hands to take his daughter back. I saw what looked like regret in Mr. Brooms' eyes, as if he wanted to keep her just a while longer. "Thank you," Mr. Brooms said quietly. "What do I owe you?"

"Not a thing," answered Uncle Alex. I couldn't figure him out. He was out of work and yet was turning down money. As I saw the look of gratitude in Mr. Brooms' eyes and the way he smiled at the baby, I started thinking that maybe some things were more important than money, like having friends and family.

"Well," said Mr. Brooms, "I could use someone to stock the shelves part-time, if you don't have anything better to do. The pay won't be too high. But maybe you can make some extra money doing repairs for a few of my business friends. Coalton doesn't have too many good repairmen since the old repair shop closed." Mr. Brooms and my Uncle shook hands.

This was great! We'd come to do a favor and left with my Uncle's first job since he'd lost the farm. But that wasn't all! Mr. Brooms turned to me and asked, "Michael, do you think your Mother would like any of these fruits and vegetables? I can't sell discolored food for full price anyhow. And, remember the crate of fruit in the back. Just clean up and toss out anything she doesn't want.

I practically killed myself hauling fruit and vegetables up the steps. I moved fast before he could change his mind. Then the best thing happened. When Uncle Alex told Momma what had happened, she took two dimes out of her coffee can bank and gave them to me. "The babies need to nap, and Anna and I have fruit to can," Momma said. "Why don't you two see what's playing at the movies?"

Sissy and I were out of the door in no time, and we didn't look back.

CHAPTER 8

RATTLESNAKE SANDWICH

Sunday went, and Monday came. It was another school day. Class went much the same as usual. I sat in the back left corner of the dimly-lit room on the sweltering third floor of Coalton Grade School. The room wasn't much to look at, but neither was the entire red brick building. Yet a lot of learning went on there.

I knew that I had learned to read and write, and I could cipher pretty well. I was one of the fastest at times tables. I knew them up through the twelves. I knew the elevens two years ago. They were pretty easy. I learned them when the price of movies in town went up to eleven cents. That was before the Depression started. It was also before Prohibition. Prohibition made whiskey and other alcohol against the law.

Before that time, kids like me could walk the area along the railroad tracks and near the river, picking up empty half pint whiskey bottles. I guess a lot of people who didn't want others to know they drank found it easy to throw their bottles into the brush. The brewery paid us a penny apiece to return them. It was cheaper for them to clean and reuse the bottles than to make new ones.

I knew that it took eleven bottles to pay for one ticket, and I knew right away how many it would take for any number of us fellows to go to the movies. All I had to do was figure my elevens.

After the Depression started, the movie houses had to lower the price to a dime to get people to go. It wasn't easy to get a dime, though. We couldn't sell back the bottles any more. It was a lot more fun when stupid people could waste their money on liquor and throw away the bottles. Then, we could go to the shows for free.

My attention came back to the classroom when the teacher came by my desk. I already knew most of what we were doing in class. Miss Millansky spent most of her time trying to help two new boys in class. One was from Slovakia and the other was from Germany. Both spoke only a little broken English, and they spoke it with heavy accents. Some of the other kids made fun of them, and there had been several fights because of it. Miss Millansky had the idea that when those two were settled in better the other thirty-six of us in the class would do better.

I hoped that was true. I wanted to learn more, but in the meantime, my mind wandered to what I would do when I took Pal to the bottoms. It was good to hear the dismissal bell ring at the end of the day.

Sissy was ready to go before I could get my books together. She stood out front of the school and waited for me. It was tempting to run past her and hurry to Grandma's house. But I was kind of getting used to having her around all the time. I was glad to hear that she was learning a lot. I told Sissy that if school didn't get any better for me, I might just quit school and get a job. Maybe with more money, Momma and Papa could afford to buy a house again, and we'd have more room to live in.

As I spoke with my sister, I realized part of the reason I wasn't learning as much. My study place at the table was always full, and there was so much noise around the house that I couldn't concentrate

We got to Grandma's in only a few minutes, and yep ... There he was. Grandpa was sitting in his rocker. His smile was one of my favorite things about him. It could make you forget everything else.

I told Grandma that I was going to take Pal on an extra long walk. We hadn't been too far lately. She told me what a good boy I was and turned to give her attention to Sissy. Grandpa called me over and winked at me. "Don't forget your candle wax." He was sharp! You couldn't fool my Grandpa! He knew exactly what I was up to. I bet if he could get around easier, he'd come right with me down to my secret spot.

Grabbing my coffee can full of wax from under the sagging corner of the porch, I called Pal. "Snort," said Pal, and away we went. I took care to stay several steps ahead of his nose in case he got any funny ideas about pulling his favorite trick on me. It only took us a few minutes to reach his tree.

While Pal was busy, I went straight to my secret spot. I put down the can of wax chunks and the candle wicking, planning to make a fire at some other time and make a huge candle out of it. I picked up my forked stick and jabbed it around inside of the hole, listened carefully for a moment, and started to step through the opening. As my left foot went in through the hole, I heard a dry rattling noise.

"Pal's done sniffing already and is here to scare me," I thought. I bent over to put my head into the hole, but before I could enter, I saw what looked like a thick rope coiled up off to my right side.

All of my senses took hold at once. I realized that the sound I heard was a rattlesnake. It sat coiled up with its head raised. With a gooseberry bush partly blocking my view, I couldn't tell how long it was. Unable to tell if I was within striking distance, I had to assume it could reach me. I stood perfectly still.

I transferred the forked stick to my right hand. Another rattling sound! My slight movement was sensed by the snake. It felt threatened and was warning me not to move. I felt obligated to listen to its warning. The problem was I couldn't stay bent over here forever. My back was staring to hurt, and my left leg was getting tired of supporting all of my weight. Beads of sweat were running down my forehead and into my eyes, but I couldn't wipe them. I had to do something soon if the snake didn't leave on its own.

I closed my eyes tightly for a second. Maybe if I didn't look at it, it would disappear. That dry shaking sound again! With my eyes closed, it sounded like pebbles shaking inside a small can. Closing my eyes hadn't worked. My eyes opened up to see the snake start to open its jaws wide. Two white fangs gleamed as its head started forward.

"Snort!" went Pal. Pal dove forward through the entrance to my secret spot and grabbed the snake's mid-section as it began to strike. The snake turned its head instantly to react to its attacker. "Move fast or lose your best friend," my mind told me!

I jammed the forked end of the stick down onto the snake's head. I pushed hard and trapped the snake between the stick and the ground like I'd seen my Grandpa do with bull snakes in the past. Pal hung on, gripping his teeth tighter and tighter. The snake convulsed and flipped its tail hard, and Pal went flying through the air.

Fear made me keep holding the stick down while I watched that fat little bull dog waddle at lightening speed right back to that snake. As Pal bit down, an arm reached past me, and a knife whacked the snake's head off! The motion of the snake's body caused the head to flip over near my feet. That's when I screamed and fell over backward with everything around me turning black!

"Easy does it," said the voice of the figure who was now standing over me. A strong hand reached out to help me to my feet. I took it and stood to see who had helped me. The man was no one that I knew, so I just stared, wondering where he'd come from. "You reacted really quickly," said the stranger.

"I had to," I answered. "You don't see many snakes down here, but my Grandpa taught me to always be prepared, especially as the weather warms up and they first start stirring. It could have bit me or my Grandpa's ..." Suddenly, I remembered Pal. I looked up, and there he was. He stood drooling over the snake's body, slobbering all over it. He was obviously very proud of himself. I really loved that dog. I reached out to pet him to say thanks. That's when he walked over to the snake's head and blew snot all over it! I wanted to laugh. But I knew I had to be careful and bury the head before Pal came near it again. The poison in a dead snake's head can still kill you.

"That's quite some dog," said the man. "You and your pet want to join me for the dinner that you helped me kill?"

"What are you talking about?" I asked, wrinkling my nose up. I wondered if he was serious or pulling my leg.

"Well, there's no sense wasting good meat! You mean you've never eaten rattlesnake before?" Then he bent over and picked up the limp body of the dead snake.

I thought he was kidding, but he wasn't. I followed him about fifty yards to a sheltered place under a tree where he had a small fire going. "I was heating myself some tea," he stated in answer to my unasked question. I got the tea bag at a restaurant earlier where I had poor man's tomato soup." He explained, "You order a cup of tea and some crackers. Then you mix ketchup and crackers with the hot tea water. It makes a passable tomato soup. Then you save the tea bag for later. But, now I've got some real meat! Tonight, I'm eating rattlesnake sandwich!" He paused, "If I can find some bread."

The man explained that he was a *bo* passing through town. We had more and more hoboes passing through, catching rides in open boxcars on the railroad. Some of the workers feel sorry for the out-of-work men and leave boxcar doors open on purpose. It's dangerous to "ride the rails" as he called it, but with so many people out of work, lots of men were desperate enough to take their chances and try to find a part of the country that had jobs.

I told him about my Grandpa's house at the top of the bottoms and how I'd come down here to make my candle. I wanted to talk more, but knew I had to get back before I was too late. I asked the man if he needed anything. He assured me that he was doing okay. He'd be moving on in the morning. He was glad he had heard Pal bark and had come to see what was happening. Believe me, so was I! I told him about my secret place in case he needed a drier place to sleep. Then, I hurried back to Grandma's before I got into big trouble.

"That was a long walk," Grandma said to me. Pal certainly seems wore out. What did you do? Chase that dog around a tree?"

"Something like that," I told Grandma. Then I let her smother me with one of her big hugs. I needed that right at that moment.

By the time I checked my secret spot again, the man had moved on. I didn't know if he had eaten his rattlesnake sandwich or not. Maybe he'd been just kidding me. There was one thing, though. Right inside the opening to my secret spot was a large red candle with a home-made wick in the center. A scribbled note read, "I needed the can for cooking, but us bo's don't take anything without working for it. Enjoy the candle."

I thought of him every time I used it!

CHAPTER 9

VOICE IN THE DARK

THE END OF SCHOOL CAME SOON after the time I'd had my scare with the snake and met my first hobo. More and more I was considering not going back to school in the fall. I even thought about running away to earn money to help my family. It bothered me terribly to watch all the adults in my home work so hard just to keep us in the dinky apartment.

It wasn't like we were starving, but in the apartment we were piled up on one another, especially at night when everyone was home. If Grandpa was not sick, Uncle Alex, Aunt Anna and Mary Elizabeth would be welcomed with love to stay with Grandpa and Grandma in their house at the top of the bottoms.

Daytime was better. Papa left early in the morning for work at the tile factory. Most summer mornings he would let me walk with him. We'd walk past Grandpa's house, stopping for coffee on the way. Secretly, Papa and Grandpa had been letting me drink coffee with milk and sugar every morning. We'd often eat Grandma's *koloche* (Czech pastries) and poppy seed rolls. It was a comfortable and happy place to be. We'd sit there, sometimes talking, sometimes in silence until the hands on Grandpa's old black clock said 6:45. Papa would get up and give Grandma a kiss on the cheek and a quick hug. He would stare for a moment at Grandpa like he wanted to do the same with him. Finally, he'd turn and head out the door.

I would call Pal and follow Papa. We'd walk beside Papa through the bottoms to the drain tile factory. It was amazing how Papa knew the names of every plant along the river bottoms and what each could be used for. He'd share things like that with me on those summer mornings. Sometimes as we walked, Papa would talk about different times in history and different places around the world. He told about them as if he'd been at every place personally, though I knew he'd learned most of his information by soaking up every word of the daily paper and the books I brought home from school. I listened eagerly as we took these daily walks. He knew far more than most other men with only an eighth-grade education.

Those morning walks were some of the only times I could have Papa to myself. The rest of the time, he was too busy with the apartment and the girls, or he was just plain tired out.

I always felt a sense of disappointment when we reached the tile factory, a spread-out single-story building close to the river. The factory was in a good place. The workers had a ready supply of red clay from the pits nearby to mold into the round pipes or tiles. More of the tiles were being bought by the government than by individual customers. The state was trying to put more farm land into use and wanted to drain swampy fields. So, more and more farmers came by to pick up tiles that the government had paid for to lay them in their fields. At any rate, there was enough business to keep Papa and the other workers employed.

Daytimes also got Uncle Alex out of the house. Daily, he went to work for Mr. Brooms. At first, he only worked for an hour or two a day. As people found out how handy Uncle Alex was with repairs, that changed. People from all over town started bringing by their old appliances for Uncle Alex to tinker with. As there wasn't room upstairs to work, Mr. Brooms let him set up an area in the back of the store for working. He could fix almost anything and enjoyed doing it. Sometimes he used his creativity to make appliances even better than when they were new.

It seemed like everyone who brought in repairs also did some shopping, so Mr. Brovotsky's store was doing more business than ever. Since he had given Uncle Alex the work area in the back of the store, the traffic into his store had increased. He was also doing more business with cash payments and less on credit, a blessing for any business during the Depression.

On one of my daily visits to the store, I overheard part of a conversation between Mr. Brovotsky and Uncle Alex. I knew it wasn't polite to listen in, but I just couldn't seem to help myself. Mr. Brovotsky was saying, "This was what I wanted all the time my son was growing up. I wanted him to help me run the store. It's not good for a man to be alone in his old age. If your brother ever moves out, I'd be glad to rent the upstairs to you. You know there's too many of you to keep living the way you are."

I didn't hear what Uncle Alex said back to him, but the problem of our crowded living situation had again been forced to the front of my mind.

Momma and Aunt Anna had even been having words with each other. Some real hostility started when Mary Elizabeth said, "Mama," when Momma picked her up.

"Overly Possessive" was what Aunt Anna had called Momma after this happened.

"Ungrateful" was what Momma had called Aunt Anna in return.

Then, the war of words became a war of glances, towels tossed rather than handed, pots banged on the counter when the two had to work together, and so on. Needless to say, Sissy spent a lot of time outside with her friends, and I spent a lot more time at the bottoms. Neither of us wanted to be at home until a truce had been declared.

Pal and I stopped by my secret place on one particularly fine day. The weather was dry and the temperature was cool. I had been tunneling away at the back of my hole, a little every day. A lot of the time, Pal stayed right with me, sometimes digging with me as my secret place turned into a mine shaft.

I had learned much about digging by talking to Grandpa. I didn't know if he realized what I was up to, but he seemed happy for the time we spent together. Grandpa talked on and on whenever I asked him questions about mining and the time he had spent digging underground. I had learned how to shore up the ceiling as I dug into the soil on the hillside. He had told me how miners put an upright support on both sides of openings, wedged tightly under a crossbeam. "Without such supports," he said one time, "half of Coalton would be caving in." Asking him further about that, he explained that most of the Vermillion River area was undermined. That meant that under every field, road, house, and store, huge strips of coal had been cut out and hauled away when the mines were still active.

I'd wanted to know where all the lumber for the supports for the mine had come from. I had been using empty fruit and vegetable crates from the store for my supports. Sometimes, I'd run short and have to wait a day or two to find more crates tossed out in the alley. Grandpa told me that lots of areas weren't supported with timbers or steel beams. Instead, they were supported by pillars of coal that the miners had left standing. Even when the mines were running out, these pillars were left in place to keep the areas above from sagging.

"It was scary," he'd said, "Some of the people in town were going into the deserted mines and cutting out these pillars of coal to heat their homes during hard times. Trouble was bound to come from it. If too many of the supports were removed, whole areas of town could cave in.

In one part of town, a woman walked out one morning only to look at her garage roof instead of the door. Grandpa claimed that sometime during the night, the entire garage had sunk about eight feet into the ground, car and all. I didn't entirely believe Grandpa, but it was a good story.

Grandpa had commented several times about how dirty Pal was. I'm sure he knew what I was up to. In fact, that morning, I'd found a shovel leaning against a tree by the path that Pal and I always took to the bottoms. Being pretty sure it had been left by Grandpa for me, I borrowed the shovel and made better progress than ever with it. I felt like a real miner as I dug my way back into the hillside through the vent opening. The soft rock and patches of clay crumbled under my blows.

Then, on one forward stroke, my shovel met almost no resistance. I couldn't figure it out for a few minutes. When I held my candle closer to the new opening I'd made, I saw that I had broken through into the old mine. I pushed my candle ahead of me as I crawled inside and looked around. It was dark and spooky, but the darkness seemed like a challenge I had to conquer. Of course, it was easier with Pal at my side.

I reached over and petted Pal. He rewarded me by snorting and spreading drool on my hand as he licked me. The two of us moved further into the mine. I just had to explore as far as I could.

I was awfully careful to mark my way so I could get back out. I thought of dropping crumbs from the poppy seed roll I'd brought with for a snack. But a delighted snort from Pal and the way he dove after the crumbs changed my mind. Instead, I dipped a stick into the soft top of my candle and smeared melted wax on the walls as Pal and I moved along.

We explored for a good amount of time. My candle made from church wax gave off a glow that looked like a halo as I walked along, so, I felt safe. In most places, I could stand up pretty easily. You could see that the seam of coal had been thick in some spots and narrow in others. There were a lot of narrow bands of coal where the miners had not even tried to cut out the coal. It probably would not have been worth their time.

It was damp in a few places, and I could see water trickling down the walls. Grandpa said that one of the deepest mines had to be abandoned when the tunnel flooded. It simply was too expensive to keep the pumps going day and night to keep the mine dry enough to remove the coal. I saw the pillars of coal Grandpa had talked about. Some of them had been chipped away so I didn't know how they could hold up the ceiling. When I saw this and started thinking about it, for the first time I felt uneasy about being down here. A picture of Grandpa's face flashed inside my mind. "Far enough," I thought.

I walked back a few feet to where I had just been and felt a sense of relief when I saw my wax mark on the wall. I sat down on the floor beside Pal. I carefully placed my candle on the floor and took a snack out of my pocket. I fed him part of the poppy seed roll, while I ate the rest. Pal then walked over to a puddle of water on the floor of the tunnel and lapped up a drink.

I watched him, envious that he could so simply meet his needs. However, I wasn't desperate enough to drink from a puddle on the floor of a coal mine. As I watched him, his ears perked up and he began to whine. It was the most mournful sound I had ever heard. Chills went through my entire body. That's when I started to get up to go. I couldn't figure out why he left me, but Pal tore back down the tunnel into the total darkness as fast as his legs could carry him. I turned around in surprise at his actions and knocked the candle against the wall.

"Hisssssss," went the candle as the water dripping down the wall hit the flame. The entire tunnel was plunged into the depths of darkness. "No worry," I thought as I reached into my pocket for the match tin. Suddenly, I realized that I had left the tin back in my secret place. Having no light to see, I held my hand up in front of my face. Although I knew it was there, I could not see it.

Drips of water seemed to be louder in the dark than they were before in the dim light. I listened for sounds of any kind, but I could only hear my own heavy breathing and the pulsing of my own heart. The absence of light caused a complete feeling of loneliness and despair. For the first time in my life, I was truly afraid for my life—not even the rattlesnake had scared me so badly.

I stopped to think. Grandpa knew where I was. He was always sitting there on his rocker to greet me when I came back. Surely, if I didn't get back, he would know to send someone to find me. I had another crazy thought, "Momma will kill me if I die down here! I've got to get out now!"

My hands went out in front of me as I tried to get a sense of where the walls were. I took each step with care. The floor that had seemed so level earlier kept rising up and dropping out from under me in the dark. I tried to remember where on the walls I had put my wax marks. Several times, I felt what I thought might be a mark, but I couldn't be certain. Further, if it was a wax mark, was it a new one or one I'd already felt. What if I was going around in circles?

Several times I stumbled. While I sat still, shivering after one of my tumbles, I thought I heard the sound of a train over my head. At one point. I thought I saw a flick of light, but when I looked again, I couldn't see anything. The mind plays terrible tricks when one is in the dark. I thought of Grandpa again. I sensed his voice calling me from the darkness ahead.

"This is it!" I said to myself. Grandpa saw Pal come home without me and came down to the bottoms to help me.

"Michael," Grandpa's voice said, "Come this way. I'm here with you, so don't be afraid. Just use your head and think your way out."

Following the voice, I put one hand ahead of me and kept one hand feeling against the side of the cave. "Shoulder height!" I remembered where my wax marks were. I had drawn wax arrows pointing back to the opening at shoulder height at two of my earlier stops. Until I'd heard Grandpa calling me, I had forgotten about this in panic. After a lot of stumbling and feeling my way, I was able to find one arrow. That told me I was going the right way.

"You're almost there," I heard the voice say. I wondered how he knew. How could Grandpa see in the dark when I could not. Then, as I felt my second arrow, I thought I saw a dim light ahead of me. After the darkness, even that dim light was nearly blinding.

I hurried to the opening, telling myself that never again was I going to enter the mines alone. I rushed to the opening, anxious to see my Grandpa and tell him thanks. Stepping outside, I felt the same chill I'd felt earlier when I'd heard Pal howl. When I looked around, Pal was nowhere to be seen, and neither was Grandpa.

Something wasn't right.

Not even bothering to wipe off the tell-tale dust, I ran back to Grandpa's. Roots of trees seemed to reach out to grab me as I raced up out of the bottoms. Out of breath, I steamed up the path that led to the top of the bottoms. I came out of the woods, into the clearing where

I'd earlier picked up the shovel, and to the house! My eyes took in the entire porch, looking for Grandpa's rocker.

The rocker was there, but it was empty.

I slowed my pace and walked steadily up the porch steps. I hoped to see Grandpa with Pal inside the house and find out what was going on. Instead, there in front of the open screen door stood Grandma. Her apron was pulled up over her face, her entire body heaving in sobs. From the inside of the house, I heard a whimper. I walked into the living room. Grandpa was laying on the davenport. Pal's head rested on Grandpa's feet. He was whining sadly. I tried to shake Grandpa, but I got no reaction. Then, Grandma came back in and wrapped her arms around me and I knew. Grandpa was dead.

CHAPTER 10

ENEMIES NO MORE

I WAS STANDING BY THE FRONT DOOR, RECEIVING THE GUESTS. People
had been pouring into Grandma's house since the wake had begun at
4:00 in the afternoon. Many faces were friends and relatives I recognized. Others were strangers to me. For example, I never knew that
Grandpa had been a member of a group called the Slovinskian Lodge.
They were a group of Russian Orthodox men who never took off their
tall black hats the entire time they were inside. I knew that more people
would continue to come until after 9:00 that night when the front lights
would be shut off.

We all had been worried about Grandma. Since her burst of tears
on the porch, Grandma had not cried or shown any sign of emotion.
She had been entirely wrapped up in preparations for the funeral.
There had been the call to the priest for Grandpa's last rites—and to
the coroner. He was called to sign the papers about the time and the
cause of death.

"Painless," was what the coroner had said. According to him,

Grandpa's tired lungs just gave out, and he died peacefully in his sleep.

Another call had been made to Mr. Solans, the undertaker, who prepared Grandpa's body for burial. Grandma had given Mr. Solans Grandpa's good suit. Papa and Uncle Alex had helped pick out the casket. The casket with Grandpa lying in it had been brought back to the house and placed in the front room for the wake. The preparations kept everyone busy.

"Tradition," was what Momma called it, when Sissy asked her about the wake. She said the body was always brought back to the house for everyone to say good-bye. Sometimes, a wake lasted for up to three days, but this one would only be one due to the intense heat of summer. Plus, no one knew how well Grandma would keep holding up.

Momma stood looking into the casket with Gertie in her arms. Aunt Anna had left earlier when Mary Elizabeth started crying and had not returned yet. Sissy mingled with the guests like the perfect young lady that Grandma needed her to be. Other than Gertie, Sissy and I were the only kids at the wake. It was mostly for grown-ups.

I knew part of the reason they didn't want kids around was because the occasion was solemn. I suspected another reason was because the men didn't want us to see how they handled their sorrow. The women cried and consoling each other, while many of the men found comfort in bottles. Several guests had brought flasks of illegal whiskey and bottles of wine with them. Despite prohibition, alcohol showed up at almost every funeral. It seemed that only when some of the men were soused could they say how they really felt. I didn't understand it.

There was more food around Grandma's house than we'd ever be able to eat. People had been very kind, bringing pies and cakes, and dishes of all kinds. Most of the people were in the dining room eating when it came to be my turn to stand as honor guard by the casket. The casket stayed open all night, and the adults took turns sitting up with the body. The casket would never be left alone until Grandpa was buried. I hadn't been alone with Grandpa since I'd left for the bottoms the day before.

ᔕ

It was so strange. Grandpa had been alive, talking to me only the day before.

.....There were so many things I wanted to tell him. He'd meant so much to me and done so much for me. I didn't know how, but he'd even saved my life in the coal mine. I didn't believe in spooks or anything, but Grandpa's thoughts were a part of me that day. And they always will be part of me.

I looked at Grandpa in the casket and touched his hand. His once-warm hand was cold and stiff to feel. But the feel didn't bother me as much as what I saw. Something about the face I had known for so many years didn't look right. When I looked carefully, I saw that it wasn't really his face that was different, but his hair. A lock of his hair had always hung down over his forehead. This had been Grandpa's attempt to hide the bald spot at the front of his scalp. I could see him in my mind as he sat on his rocker outside, hair hanging down over his forehead and his pipe clenched in his teeth.

I tried to smooth the hair into place with my fingers, but it wouldn't stay. That's when I did something I probably shouldn't have done. I went into the dining room and got a pat of butter. I also picked up Grandpa's pipe from where it sat, along with Grandpa's tobacco pouch. Grandma had not been able to bring herself to put them away before the wake.

I reached into the casket and smeared a little of the butter on the top of Grandpa's head to make his hair stay in place when I combed it the right way, and then I put his pipe in his hand and his tobacco pouch into his suit pocket. This was the way I wanted to remember Grandpa.

I started crying. For the first time I understood why those men were drinking. They were trying to hold back the hurt.

I was glad when it came to be someone else's turn to stand the honor guard. I walked quickly out of the room after saying my good-byes and went into the dining room. I spotted something that took away my tears.… The Shinsky Sisters walked through the front door.

Emma and Edna Shinsky were two old maids who lived in Coalton. They never missed a wake or a funeral. Emma, at one time, had been the secretary for Coalton's one lawyer. Her sister, Edna, had been a desk nurse at the hospital. Between the two, they had known a lot of people in their day. As they got older, they found themselves going to a lot of funerals. After all, Emma had drawn up nearly all of the wills for families all over town, so Edna had inside information about everyone at the hospital who might be passing on.

It may have started out innocently, but the two were notorious funeral crashers. They no longer knew the deceased half of the time, but they mourned with the best of them anyhow. People said that they dressed in their black silk dresses and white gloves wherever they went. Their white handkerchiefs were wiping their eyes every time the hearse went by.

As I entered the dining room, I knew we were in for some trouble. Only two things could have brought Grandma to a boil. One was the sight of Pal in the house. However, we'd tied him out back, so Grandma didn't make good her threat and get rid of him. The other was the Shinsky sisters. Grandma had said earlier that if the two old free-loaders came to the door, she would throw them out with her own two hands. I got Sissy. Then the two of us took a good seat and waited for the excitement to begin.

We watched the two sisters go into action. They were smooth. Emma would make two sandwiches, one for her and one for her sister, wrapping both in napkins. Next, she'd lean over the table and pick up something else, accidentally knocking the sandwiches into her open purse. Edna wasn't nearly so sneaky. She heavily buttered rolls, put thick pieces of carved ham between them, and put them into her pockets. Apples and plums disappeared right in front of people's eyes and showed up as bulges in the sisters' large handbags. Emma was beginning to lean heavily to one side and would have to add more food to the other side to balance herself before long.

Then, Grandma caught sight of them. She had been at the casket where Father Zarecki had just finished leading part of the family in saying the Rosary. He would be the one to say the Mass at the funeral tomorrow also. Grandma still had her prayer beads in her hands when she caught sight of the Shinsky sisters. She soon began to make up for her lack of emotion earlier. Steam was building up inside of her, and a glaze was forming over her eyes.

Papa and Uncle Alex saw her and started walking her way. I think the give-away was when she wrapped the wooden Rosary beads around her hand and made a fist. She began stalking them to see which way they had gone and take out her frustration on them. I didn't know what would happen when Grandma found them, but the fur was going to fly.

The only other exciting thing that could happen did. Pal came bursting through the front door as a group of visitors walked out. He had been kept out of the excitement too long and was ready to make up for it all in one moment.

Grandma had waxed the floors earlier while preparing for the wake. So, when Pal came running around the corner and into the dining room, his feet flew out from under him. Snorting and drooling, he slid across the floor and into Grandma's feet. Grandma reacted by booting the dog with the side of her foot. She intended to deal with him later, having two other victims to take her anger out on first.

There were the sisters in all their glory. Their handbags were full of food and their pockets were bulging. Both were slowly shuffling toward the door, ready to escape with their booty. Grandma stepped briskly, and moved directly into their path.

That's when Pal appeared between the sisters and their exit to freedom. The two ladies stopped and gazed at the dog. Grandma stood ready to take on all three at once. Pal sized up Grandma and evidently chose sides in the event. He pranced up to the Shinsky sisters and blew snot all over their feet.

Grandma stepped out of their path as they dripped their way to the back door of the house, heading the opposite direction from the dog. Funerals would never be the same for them again. There would always be an element of fear to curb their enjoyment.

For Grandma, the sting and hurt of Grandpa's loss disappeared at least for a moment. She knew Grandpa would have appreciated how Pal defended her home. Grandma cut a chunk of ham and gave it to Pal, along with a saucer of milk, which he quickly lapped up before a satisfied burp.

"Maybe I'll keep you around here after all," she said, and then went back to be with her guests until the wake was over.

CHAPTER 11

PIG'S FEET JELLO

OUR STRONG-WILLED GRANDMA FINALLY REACTED to Grandpa's absence. She refused to be alone in her house. Day and night, she stayed at the apartment with us. If the family went out, Grandma went out. If we stayed in, Grandma stayed in. She started acting upset even if Sissy and I wanted to go outside and walk the dog. It was like if we left her sight, we might disappear forever. Even at night, everything we did was for Grandma. I gave up my bed on the couch to Sissy, and I slept on the floor. Grandma then took her bed. As much as I loved Grandma, this was getting to be too much! Everyone was getting on each others' nerves.

Only Pal got to escape the crowding. He took to sleeping outside on the porch to avoid being climbed on and chewed on by the two little ones. It was funny that a creature who spent all of his extra time drooling and slobbering couldn't stand two messy babies.

To make things worse for us in the apartment, Grandma had an urge to cook for everyone. That would not have been too bad if

Grandma was a meat and potatoes person. But, No! That would have been too normal. Since she'd come to live with us, she had to do everything the old fashioned way. She dug out an old Czech cookbook that her mother had brought over from the old country. It was like she was trying to relive the past by trying all these odd recipes that some family member had written down long ago. Some weren't too bad, but these weren't the ones that Grandma wanted to try right then.

Grandma sent me downstairs to Mr. Brovotsky's store to buy pigs' feet. She wanted to make pigs' feet jello. Pal thought this was great, somewhere new to go. He tried following me into the store, but Mr. Brovotsky's broom found a new use. You could tell that Pal wanted to take his revenge on the instrument that had hurt his pride and swept him out of the store. But at the first sign of his sniffing around, Mr. Brovotsky swatted him again. Pal saw that he wasn't going to get anywhere and left to go around to the alley and sulk. Both Mr. Brovotsky and I stood there laughing. It was funny to see Pal lose a battle to a broom.

I walked back to the meat counter. Half of a beef carcass was hanging from an overhead hook. Various cuts of pork were displayed, including a selection of pigs' feet. They were ugly. The hooves were still on them, and little tufts of hair stuck out of them. They didn't appear to have much meat at all on them. But one thing, they were cheap. Mr. Brovotsky wrapped the pigs' feet in brown paper and tied a string around the package for me. I asked him to please put the bill on our tab. Momma always settled our account at the end of the month. Then, I went back upstairs.

Pal gave me a dirty look and snorted at me as I passed him on the porch. It was like I was a traitor for staying in the store where he wasn't allowed. I went inside and gave the package to Grandma. Then, I got Sissy and told her what Grandma was cooking. At first, Sissy, who was by then getting tired of being the perfect lady, and I watched with interest. After a bit, however, we started to wish Grandma had never found that cookbook while going through things back at her house.

Grandma chased Momma and Aunt Anna out of the kitchen. The two had patched up their differences. Now, they had a common enemy, Grandma. Grandma turned on the propane gas tank behind the stove. (She'd started turning it off when the stove wasn't in use. This drove Momma nuts.) "Not safe, these modern inventions," Grandma said. "You never can be too careful. There might be a leak in the gas line to the stove."

Gas on. Burner turned up. Match lit—and poof! The flame ignited. Grandma turned up the flame until it shot nearly a foot in the air. *And she said that Momma wasn't safe?*

Grandma speared the pigs' feet with a metal skewer. "Watch this," she said to Sissy. "You've got to learn how to fix fine food for your husband." Sissy didn't want to talk about husbands and wasn't really thrilled about having Grandma teach her to cook. But she sat there politely, still curious what Grandma was up to. We watched with our eyes wide open as she held the pigs' feet over the high flame to burn the hair off the knuckles. A stench permeated the room. Watching this might not have been the best idea after all.

"When the skin around the pigs' feet char and turn black, they'll be ready to boil. Charring them," Grandma said with enthusiasm, "locks the flavor in." Sissy and I looked at each other and both stuck out our tongues at almost the same time as Grandma went on with her back to us. "Nothing is as good as sucking the juice out of a well-cooked pig's foot and chewing on the gristle." As she said that, my stomach suddenly didn't feel too well.

She put the pigs' feet into a large pot on the stove and filled it with water. "These will have to boil almost all day. When the hooves are almost dissolved, they'll be done cooking, and then, all we have to do is let the mixture cool until the fat turns solid like jello. You two will get the first bites since you've been nice enough to stay and watch me make it." Grandma said.

That was it. Sissy and I decided to run away. *No one was going to make us eat pigs' feet jello,* I thought, *pigs' feet—of course, Grandma's pig!*

"Momma," I pleaded with a sense of urgency. She came into the kitchen for a moment. "No one has fed Grandma's pig for the last few days." I think Momma knew I needed to get away from here and consented to let me go. Sissy looked at me with her big eyes, begging. "And can Sissy go too?" I added. "I'll need help carrying the slop bucket."

My last comment wasn't true, and Momma knew it. I'd been carrying heavy loads of scraps to Grandma's for a long time, but she said that it would be a good idea. She packed Sissy and me a picnic lunch. It was like she was rewarding me for giving Sissy the chance to escape the house with me. Grateful for our freedom, Sissy and I loaded all the scraps we could find in our garbage and from the alley behind the store, into buckets we'd put into our old red wooden wagon. We quickly left the apartment and did all we could to forget about Grandma's cooking.

Pal decided to forgive me and rubbed his wet nose on my pant leg. He snorted a few times until I stopped and reached down to pet him.

"I can't take this any more," I told Sissy. "I've got to do something to help. We can't all stay in one apartment without everyone going nuts. And Grandma's not helping!"

"That's no news to me," my sister reminded me. "I'm the one that Grandma keeps trying to turn into the perfect wife for someone, and I don't want to get married. At least not for years. I want to do something real with my life."

I thought that was a silly thing to say. What else was there for a girl to do but to get married, but then I thought, "Why not? If any girl was going to do something great, it might as well be my sister.

We talked until we made it to Grandma's house. Pal automatically started for his tree down in the bottoms. I guess he thought I was with him. He went part way down the path and then came back to snort at me for not going with him. I bent down to pet him, and he took in a deep breath of air. I got far away from him before he could play his snot-blowing trick on me. Anyway, Sissy and I had work to do. We walked around the house and saw Grandma's pig rooting, trying to dig under the fence that separated the pen from the side of the ravine. If that pig had succeeded, it could have fallen and died, since a drop-off at that point fell about sixty feet down to the bottoms. Sissy saw the pig digging and started right through the gate to stop it. Pal squeezed through the gate before it could shut, having decided Sissy need a companion.

"No!" I screamed, running into the pen. Sissy didn't hear me and kept on walking. I heard the gate shut behind me as I ran towards her. Before Sissy could defend herself, that pig squealed with an insane cry and charged my sister. Its head was low to the ground and its mouth was open, baring ragged teeth as it charged. Pal stepped between the charging animal and Sissy. The pig tripped over Pal's fat body, caught its balance and continued to charge towards its original target.

Sissy stood as if rooted to the ground, unable to move. Summoning strength from somewhere, I picked up my sister and threw her over the fence rail toward the house. Then, I started running back towards the gate. I heard Pal get up, shake himself off, and snap at the pig. Pal was not one to take being knocked around lightly.

"What's the matter with you, you moron?" Sissy yelled angrily after landing in a pile of mud. Scooping up a handful of the muck to throw it at me, she suddenly noticed the pig charging me—and screamed. When I heard her, I knew that I'd been right to run!

I didn't have to look back to know the pig was after me. I could hear the heavy grunts and feel the ground shake behind me as I tried to stay one step ahead of it. With the menacing pig hot on my heels, I realized I wouldn't be able to get to the gate in time to open it up and get out. As I leaped for the top rail, Grandma's old pig grabbed the heel of my shoe. I got out of the pen all right. But, when I looked at my shoe, it was missing a chunk of the heel.

That could have been my foot!

I looked back into the pen to see that Pal was in trouble. Unable to catch Sissy or me, the crazy pig was going after Pal. I grabbed a handful of scraps, pelting the side of the pig with rotten potato peels and onion rings. He hesitated for a few seconds. While he did, I opened the gate. I didn't have to call Pal. He had seen the gate move, and definitely wanted out. The pig also saw the open gate, and the race was on. Pal reached it a second before the pig, and I managed to shut the gate just in time. Then, I threw my weight against the gate and held it while Sissy fastened the latch.

∽

"What happened to Grandma's pig?" she asked me. "It's never been wild before."

I couldn't answer for a few moments. I had to catch my breath after my second close call. I laid back on a patch of bare grass and reclined, panting. Pal fell down beside me with his head on my ankles.

When I caught my breath, I answered my sister, "That's what happens when they're left to starve. I think she went a little crazy. They do the same thing when they have a litter of piglets. They get a lot meaner for a while. It's not the pig's fault, she's just hungry." When we both caught our breath, we began to toss the scraps we'd brought toward the pig's trough from outside the fence. We weren't going inside the gate not even to give that pig water until we were sure she was at least halfway full from the scraps we'd brought.

I let Sissy throw the scraps into the pen for a moment while I looked at my shoe. If he'd only torn the heel off, I could have gotten a new heel from the cobbler. But the shoe had a chunk of leather torn off above the heel. As my fingers explored the shoe, they also touched the back of my foot. It was wet. When I held my fingers up and looked at them, I saw the red of my own blood. It was an uncomfortable feeling. When I took my stocking off, I found a small nick where one of the pig's sharp teeth had broken through my skin. I wasn't hurt, but it bothered me to know how close she had come to catching me. It bothered me that I would have to wear those torn shoes for a few months, since we only bought new shoes once a year. My next pair wouldn't come until the start of school.

Sissy and I did our part, feeding and watering Grandma's future bacon supply.

Afterward, Sissy and I decided to find a way to get cleaned up for our picnic. We really didn't want to go home yet, so we looked over the outside of the house, trying to find an excuse to go inside and explore without adults around to tell us what we couldn't touch. It was Sissy who suggested that my wound needed care. I Thought I should probably get some iodine to put on my cut. Of course, the only iodine nearby was in the house. If that didn't work, I could always tell Momma that we were checking to see if the house was locked up tight. I climbed the trellis to the second story. Grandma had locked up the downstairs part of the house well. However, she'd forgotten to lock the upstairs windows.

I crawled through a window that Grandma had left ajar and shut it behind me. Downstairs in a flash, I opened the door for Sissy. The house felt so empty. "It's so quiet," I whispered to Sissy.

"And so big!" we said simultaneously. We looked at each other with big eyes. We were both thinking the exact same thing. If Grandma didn't want to be alone, why didn't we try to get Momma and Papa to move with us into Grandma's house? We could keep her company! Uncle Alex and Aunt Anna could keep the apartment. All we had to do was to plan our case and present it convincingly. During the trip to the bottoms, we talked about how to explain our ideas to the adults. I didn't want Pal to think we'd totally forgotten about what he wanted.

"Not a bad idea at all, Papa said later that evening when we told our idea to him. Even Momma liked it. Grandma could have her old room. Momma and Papa could have a bedroom, and Sissy and Gertie could have the other. I'd take the sewing room upstairs for my room, I suggested. Sissy was willing to accept this—for now. She was pretty sure she could get Papa to turn part of the attic space into a room for her later.

Everyone knew it would work, including Uncle Alex and Aunt Anna. It still wouldn't be a home of her own for Momma, but she would have a full-sized kitchen. We'd be sharing a whole house, instead of an apartment. "All we have to do is get Grandma to agree," I said.

"Grandma already agrees," said a voice from the other room. Grandma had been listening the entire time. "Now all we have to do is celebrate. And—I've got the perfect way to do it," beamed Grandma. "In fact, the two who came up with the idea get the first helping. Come on in for dinner. We're having Pigs' Feet Jello!"

Sissy and I groaned.

CHAPTER 12

GREEN FOAM AND A STAGGERING SOW

WE HAD BEEN LIVING IN GRANDMA'S HOUSE FOR ABOUT A MONTH when the most horrible smell wafted up from the bottoms. Sissy and I looked straight at Gertie. She had been out of diapers and into regular pants for a long time, but that smell was still familiar to us! She was our prime suspect for the stink in the air. But when we looked her way, she was holding her nose too. So, we believed she might be innocent after all. The smell invading our noses was so bad that our eyes were watering. It was even affecting Pal, who laid down on the porch and covered his nose with both paws.

The three of us kids walked out back, past the pig pen. Whatever was causing the smell had the interest of the pig too. Grandma's pig was straining to get through the fence at whatever was causing the offensive odor. We stood for a time watching the pig press her nose between white pickets of the fence. She would sniff for a while, and then go a bit crazy. That old pig ran back and forth, then stopped to dig with her hooves at the bottom of the structure that was holding her back from what must have seemed to her to be piggy heaven. Grunts and squeals filled the air.

As we stood there, Momma left her clothesline and came our way. The clothes flapped in the breeze, which was carrying the almost sickening sour smell. I hoped that my shirts wouldn't pick up the smell, causing me to be embarrassed in school, which started the next week. Momma walked right over to where we were standing. She didn't seem to have the questioning look on her face that my sisters had. It was like she knew what the smell was. Her right arm reached out and we looked where her finger pointed.

We watched as a fuzzy grayed head appeared at the crest of the hill. A faded blue sweater could be seen a few minutes later, a sweater that we knew belonged to Grandma. She came straight toward us at a pace faster than she had walked in weeks. Everyone could see the ear to ear smile on Grandma's red face.

"Cabbage is ripe," was all we could hear her say above the rustle of the trees around her.

"Cabbage!!!" Now we all knew what the smell was. Grandma had often planted cabbage in the fertile bottomland. She cooked it for Grandpa, who admired cooked cabbage almost as much as apple pie. The rest of us wondered what she'd had put in the cabbage plants this year.

Grandma was huffing and out of breath by the time she reached us. The fast pace up the hill had taken its toll on her old legs, and she was becoming unsteady as she walked. "Michael," Momma said in her "God" voice, the one she reserved for serious trouble. I knew what she wanted right away and hurried over to Grandma's side.

"I'm glad to know what that smell is, Grandma," I said. My right arm tried to slip around her bulky waist as I talked, making it look like a hug. I couldn't reach far enough to give Grandma the support she needed and looked pleadingly at Sissy. She picked up on my glance and ran to Grandma's other side. We both hooked her arms and loved her to death, all the way to the rocker on the front porch next to where Pal still laid without budging.

Momma watched our every move. The nodding of her head up and down told us that we'd both been right to leave Grandma her pride and not say anything about her near-fall. Grandma sat down heavily on the rocker and leaned her head forward. After Momma saw Grandma was all right, she returned to her clothes on the line. Gertie started to climb into Grandma's lap, but I scooped her up and swung her around and around. Sissy ran into the house for a moment, but Gertie and I ignored her and kept up our play. I held Gertie's wrists in my hands carefully as she started her run. Over and over, I twirled around, matching her speed and lifting Gertie gently upward as I continued turning. Her eyes looked up at me as her feet flew straight out. As we turned, I tried to keep my eyes on Grandma. After a few moments of turning, it wasn't easy to focus on anything. I was getting so dizzy that I had to stop.

Gertie ran off to tell Momma that I wouldn't play with her anymore. I plopped down on the porch in time to see the color start to come back into Grandma's face. Her head raised up when the slamming of the screen door announced Sissy's return to the porch. Sissy came toward us carrying a pitcher and five glasses on a tray. Pal's eyes opened for a moment, and shut again when he saw there was nothing for him on the tray.

Grandma called to Momma. When she and Gertie sat down on the porch steps, Sissy poured everyone a tall glass of lemonade. We sat in silence as Grandma pointed toward the bottoms. "Force of habit," was all Grandma said for a few minutes. Her eyes became a bit glazed as she sat before us. She wiped away a tear that had started to form at the corner of her eye. "Darn cabbage," said Grandma, "It stinks so bad; it's making my eyes water. "Grandpa had always loved his cabbage. We planted it every year. In his younger days, Grandpa had tried to plant corn in the bottoms. It grew really well in the years when the floods didn't wash the seeds away. The old river coons kept getting at it though, so he eventually gave up on the corn. We still kept planting cabbage year after year. The coons left it alone, and all the dogs in the bottoms kept the bunnies at bay."

We expected to hear her say more, but she remained quiet for a moment. Suddenly, with a burst of new energy, she leaned forward in the rocker and almost sprang out of the chair. "Time to make sauerkraut," Grandma blurted out with enthusiasm. "EVERYONE gets to help." Pal sat up for the first time that day and snorted as if to agree with Grandma.

❧

The next day nearly everyone got into the action. Uncle Alex was working at the store with Mr. Brooms. Aunt Anna, who had come over, kept Gertie busy helping her watch the baby. Pal ran around, excited to have company, then sat down to help watch the baby too. Actually, he sat there expectantly because the baby had a habit of throwing everything, including food, onto the ground by her feet. Pal was only too happy to help her clean it up.

Papa had the day off, since it was Saturday, so he and I did most of the smelliest work. We used long butcher knives to cut the cabbages from their stems. It wasn't hard to cut the cabbage, but it was messy and stinky.

After we cut the heads, we had to strip off the rotting, brown outer leaves from the firm round heads of cabbage. This was disgusting work. We piled them up and, later, carried them up the hill to feed to the pig. Nothing was allowed to go to waste. We pulled up the roots, shook the dirt off, and tossed them into the pig pen on other trips to the top of the bottoms.

Papa and I washed the slime and the mud off of ourselves at the pump before carrying the cabbages in to the women. This was done at Grandma's direction. She wasn't about to have her sauerkraut spoiled by letting dirt or rot get into it. The feel of the cold water on my bare arms made my whole body shiver. When my hands were clean, I cupped them beneath the water as Papa continued to pump. Nothing was ever so good as an icy drink of water on a hot day when the pump had been working for a long time. When we'd had our fill of cold water, Papa and I took several of Grandma's flour sacks down to the waiting heads of cabbage.

It was funny to see Papa handle each head of cabbage with such care. I started to toss mine into a sack, when he reminded me that Grandma had said to handle them carefully. Then, he looked over his shoulder. It was almost like he could remember some time in the past when she'd followed him to the bottom to be sure he'd done the task as directed. It was fun trying to picture Papa as a boy. All too soon, the moment passed. The sacks were full, and the hard trip up the path to the top had to be made. Papa hoisted a sack in each arm and flipped them over his shoulder with ease. The full bags hung over his back reminding me of Christmas cards pictures of Santa's pack of toys. I struggled with my one sack, but I kept up with his giant strides as he climbed to the pump, where Grandma waited.

The image of Christmas continued as he sat his sacks by Grandma. She pulled the heads of cabbage out of the sacks and one by one rolled them over in her hands as if each was a special present. Each head of cabbage was ceremoniously washed thoroughly and handed over to Momma and Sissy for their part of the work.

Sissy got a job that I wouldn't want. She inspected each head to pull off any cabbage worms that were dumb enough to stay around and get caught. The rest, Momma said, would float to the top in the Kraut barrel. We could pick them out later. I was grossed out by the thought that some of the worms might not be found. Concentrating, I dismissed this thought from my mind. We would find them all, and that was that.

Grandma and Momma used long knives on a cutting board to shred the cabbage. The shredded cabbage was packed into a clean, watertight wooden barrel. After every several cabbages had been added to the barrel, Grandma added just the right amount of salt to both flavor and preserve the cabbage. Both women cut and chopped until their arms were tired. They had just sat down to rest for a moment when Uncle Alex arrived at the house. It turned out that he had been busy in his repair shop instead of working for Mr. Brooms. He had fixed Grandma's shredder.

The shredder was a wooden board with a blade placed into it. The blade was angled into the board so that vegetables pushed across the flat board were automatically sliced. The height of the blade could be adjusted according to whatever thickness was desired. Grandpa had originally designed the shredder for Grandma, but she had worn it out and tossed it into the junk pile. Uncle Alex couldn't resist the challenge of fixing and improving it. He had added sides that stuck up to keep vegetables from falling off the cutting board. He also had invented a device with a handle that could be used to press the vegetables down the board safely as they were shredded. He showed Grandma how it could be used to stop the finger wounds that had previously gone along with making sauerkraut and putting up other vegetables.

A hug from Grandma was all the payment Uncle Alex wanted and needed. After a quick lesson, we all took turns shredding the remaining heads of cabbage. Even Papa took part in what was usually considered women's work. Times were a' changing!

❧

In almost no time, the barrel was filled. Then came the hard part, pressing the cabbage. Grandma had a wooden handle with a flat end at the bottom. She used it as a press to pack the cabbage tightly into the barrel. To make sauerkraut, it was necessary to press most of the water out of the shredded cabbage. The salt helped draw the liquid out of the strings of cabbage, which Grandma called *slaw*.

The slaw had to be pressed tightly, kept under a layer of water that formed on top, and allowed to actually rot in the barrel. A small board with a brick on top of it helped keep a layer of liquid over the slaw. The thin layer of water kept the air out so it didn't spoil. A cloth was placed over the barrel to keep flies and dirt out. I asked Grandma why she didn't put the wooden lid on top of the barrel. She responded by telling me that the cabbage had to breathe. This confused me, but I didn't ask her anymore.

The first day, only a little water rose to the top. Along with the water came a few worms, like Momma had predicted. She scraped them off in a hurry and threw into them into the pigpen. The pig gobbled them down with delight. That old pig was constantly rooting around looking for such treats.

It became one of my jobs to press the sour smelling cabbage daily. The stink kept getting worse each time I did it, and after a few days, green foam started floating to the top. Grandma said the cabbage was "working." I didn't know what she meant, but I began to take more of an interest in this job that I had disliked at first. The little bits of green foam that Grandma scraped off were quickly tossed off the side of the ravine, where rain would wash it into the bottoms. I thought this was strange, since the rest of the garbage was fed to the pig.

After a few days of supervision, Grandma decided I could press the kraut by myself. That's when I got an idea. When I pressed down in one spot, the cabbage would pop up in another spot. So, I got the idea of cutting down the size of the barrel lid to press down the cabbage all at once. I put the lid onto the top of the barrel, and it fit wonderfully. Just as I was trying to think of something to press down the lid with, along came Sissy. A gleam came to her eyes when she heard my suggestion.

In no time at all, I picked up barefooted Sissy and stood her on the barrel lid, while I held her to keep her from falling over. The press worked. Sissy's weight caused more of the green foam to come to the top that ever before. I didn't know how Sissy would ever get the smell off her feet, however. After helping my sister down, we talked to each other about what to do with the foam. Sissy said to throw it into the garbage like Grandma always did. But being taught not to waste anything, I convinced Sissy the foam should be fed to the pig.

You have never seen a pig so happy! She attacked the foam faster than she'd ever gone after her slop. Then, the strangest thing happened. A few minutes after lapping up the last of the foam, the pig began running around the pen squealing at the top of her voice. Her grunts and squeals sounded almost like music. She started staggering and running into things. Finally, she leaned up against her trough, hiccuped, licked the bottom, and fell over snoring. Sissy and I laughed in hysterics and ran into the house to share what had happened.

"You crazy kids," Grandma half laughed as she scolded us. "That foam was fermented cabbage. When the salted cabbage rots to become sauerkraut, the waste product becomes alcohol. What you two did was to make that old pig drunk."

Sissy and I were worried that someone might find out and call the law on us, since Prohibition made the serving of alcohol illegal. We didn't know if that included pigs.

CHAPTER 13

PURPLE FEET

Sissy and I were back in school before we knew it. I left Miss Millanski's room to become a sixth-grader in Mrs. Honniger's Room. I was back into the routine of going to school during the day, doing homework at night, and sneaking some playtime in between homework, dog walking, and chores.

Five days a week, Sissy walked with me from Grandma's house at the top of the bottoms, up the hill to school. For Sissy, this was the best thing that could have happened. She was able to leave the world of cooking, cleaning, and childcare and enter the world of dreams. "I want to be a doctor," she announced one day. Then, "Instead of a doctor, I want to own my own business," Sissy proudly announced the next. She always dreamed big dreams.

I liked to listen to her jabber on and on as we walked to and from school. She played well with the other girls, using old farm twine to jump rope. Luckily, she hadn't reached the age yet where her class-mates would notice that she wore hand-me-downs that Momma had gotten from Father Zarecki at church. New clothes cost too much, and Momma was focused on saving enough money for a house of our own. Most of the other girls wore hand-me-downs, too. The Depression made life rough on the families in town and on the farms. Often, children's clothes came from older siblings. A cotton dress or pair of blue jeans could be worn by three or four siblings or passed from one family to another.

"Michael, how come Grandma is so weird about school?," she asked me as we walked homeward.

I knew what she was talking about. I remembered Grandma telling her the night before, "It'll never happen!" That was Grandma's response to Sissy's latest dream about what to do when she grew up. "It'll never happen," Grandma said as she shook her jowls from side to side and rolled her eyes. "Enjoy this learning while you can. It'll help you be a better wife, so you can help your husband someday with his work."

Momma hadn't said anything for fear of hurting my sister's feelings, but I knew she felt the same. She knew Sissy would grow up and accept her role as a woman some day. Momma had given up on her own dreams when she married our daddy. She had figured out that women belonged in the home Yet, Momma let Sissy dream on, rather than pop her bubble now. Besides, Momma had more to think about than Sissy's education. She was still upset about a letter Uncle Alex had shared with Papa.

The bank had notified Uncle Alex of the status of the lien against the farm in Wisconsin. The crop planted by the sharecropper had kept the bills from piling up higher. However there was still the matter of interest. If the back interest wasn't paid by the end of December, the farm would be sold to pay the bank, no questions asked!

～

"Michael," Sissy nudged me back out of my dreams. "I asked how come Grandma doesn't like school." Sissy stared at me demanding an answer.

"She's old fashioned," I said. "Remember, she only went to school through sixth grade. She can read the Bible and her recipe books. Grandpa always read the newspaper out loud if anything good was in it. That was good enough for her." As I spoke, I noticed Sissy's eyes drop towards the ground. I continued, "But, look at Momma! She graduated from the eighth grade. She learned enough to help Papa with his books before the business went under."

Sissy's eyes still focused on the ground, and I could tell that the thought of not completing school was hurting her. "But, you know times are changing. Heck, you'll graduate from high school and be able to do anything you set your mind to."

Sissy looked up and grinned. I guess I had said the right thing. She started jabbering about how she was going to be a movie actress just like Marlene Dietrich. I laughed out loud at that comment. A fellow could only be nice to his sister so long after all. As I stood doubled over laughing at the thought that my sister could ever consider herself as gorgeous as Marlene Dietrich, Sissy walked off into the bushes. I saw her going out of the corner of my eye and started to walk towards the opening where she disappeared.

Just as I stepped into the opening where she'd gone, I heard a whizzing sound coming toward me. Then, *splat*! Right on my forehead! Purple dripped down my face. The aroma of ripe grapes had escaped me earlier, but my nostrils were smelling it now.

How could I not smell it? My own sister had splattered my face with an entire bunch of grapes.

My first inclination was to return her fire with a "grapeshot" volley of my own. Then responsibility took over again, and I thought of what Momma could do with ripe grapes: grape pie, grape jam, grape Juice, and maybe a little bit of Grandma's "communion wine," as she called it.

Sissy had both hands full of ammunition, expecting her first shot to bring me into a battle for which she was well prepared.

"Truce," I called. "I surrender."

Sissy stood firmly rooted, ready to fire, just in case I was fibbing. When she was certain that I wasn't going to come after her, she celebrated her victory by tipping back her head and popping one after another of the round purple fruits into her mouth. Eyes closed, she stood there, smacking her lips, enjoying every drop of the juicy treats, as they burst open under the gentle pressure of her teeth.

"Let's tell Momma about the grapes," I suggested. "There's a million things she and Grandma can do with them." As I spoke, I looked around. These weren't just wild grapes. They were covering a huge arbor that extended for nearly a half of a block behind the bushes, hidden from the roadway. Some unfortunate property owner had spent a long time planting and tending them, only to lose the land and have to move away. Stories like this were common nowadays, but, their loss was our gain. It wouldn't be stealing after all if all we did was to keep some old grapes from being wasted.

Sissy suggested that we surprise Momma and Grandma by coming back after supper and picking them by ourselves. The look of happiness on her face convinced me that her idea made perfectly good sense. I could just picture Momma and Grandma when we did an extra chore to provide for the family without being told to. Therefore, we raced home to eat and do our assigned chores.

It was still early enough in the school year that I didn't have a lot of homework, so that night was perfect for picking grapes. Momma kept looking at the two of us funny. She must have figured we weren't causing any trouble, because she left us alone. We didn't even have to help clean up the supper dishes that night. Telling Momma we'd be home by dark, we ran to the shed to get the old red wagon.

Sissy sometimes had problems with chigger bites when she helped with things like picking grapes or other chores that required us to get into bushes or deep grass. I couldn't understand how bugs too small for me to see could bite and cause her to itch so much, but we prepared for them before leaving the shed. I dipped strips of torn up cloth into some kerosene that Grandma kept for her old hurricane lamps; she still didn't trust the electric lights that Grandpa had insisted they install in the house. Then, Sissy tied the wet strips of cloth around her ankles and wrists. The smell of the kerosene was supposed to keep the chiggers away. I didn't know if it would work with them, but I knew the stink would keep *me* from getting too close to her. I loaded two large wooden barrels onto the old wagon we kept in the shed. Sissy helped to balance the barrels as I pulled the old Western Flyer down the road as rapidly as we could go.

Before we knew it, we were back at our own personal vineyard, ready to harvest our find. I pulled and yanked on the vines until juice was running down both arms. Then, I started using my pocket knife to cut the stems of bunch after bunch of the fragrant smelling grapes. Sissy, meanwhile, effortlessly pinched one bunch after another off the vines and dropped them into her barrel. There was still a lot of green left on some of the bunches, but we picked them anyway. Anyone who makes jam knows that a few green ones are necessary to help the jam turn more solid without adding any store bought stuff to the grapes and sugar. We worked fast and furious to get all of the grapes picked before it got too dark to see. Pal walked up and snorted at me as I put the last bunch of grapes into my barrel.

We loaded our harvest onto the wagon and struggled to get it home before Momma came hunting for us. As we pulled the wagon into the shed, we saw Momma standing on the front porch. Her arms were folded and her foot was tapping. I sent Sissy right into the house as soon as she had taken her rags off of her wrists and ankles. Then, I took a couple of pieces of cheese cloth and put them over the grapes to keep the bugs out until we could work with them the next day and went into the house.

If Momma had any indication about what we were up to, she didn't mention it. She just scooted us straight to the sink to wash up and headed us off to bed.

The entire next day, I had trouble concentrating on my work at school. More than once, I found myself looking forward to getting home and working with the grapes. I couldn't tell anyone, though, because all the guys would tease me about doing women's work.

❧

The end of the school day finally came, and the three o'clock bell rang. In the mad rush for the door, I ran right into John Edward Branshuk, the banker's son. I was surprised that he spoke to me. I didn't usually run in the same circle as John Edward and his friends. I half-listened as I kept slowly walking out of the classroom door and towards the stairway.

"Michael," he said to me. "You're good at building, aren't you?" He looked around as if to see if the teacher or anyone else could hear him.

"I can build about anything," I answered. I was pretty proud of being able to work with my hands and felt proud that my talents were noticed by others. "Why do you want to know?" I asked suspiciously.

John Edward looked around again. Then he said, "Some of the others are going to join me down by the river later. We're building a fort down near the bottoms over by the bend in the river."

That sounded like fun to me. So, I stopped and gave John Edwards my full attention.

"We're tearing apart the old mining company bridge to get materials to build with. No one even goes near the old bridge anymore. The trains can't use it because of the way the river has eroded the banks under it."

Building sounded like fun to me, but I figured I'd better talk to Papa later to be sure it was okay to tear down the company bridge. I wanted to be part of their group, but I didn't want to end up in reform school if I got caught breaking the law. "I've got chores to do tonight, but I might join you tomorrow after school, if that's okay," I said.

"Your loss for tonight," said John Edwards. We might not still be interested in having you join us tomorrow. We'll see." Then, he tossed his head back, put his nose in the air, and stomped off.

It was tempting to run after him, but as I reached the exit to the school, I saw Sissy waiting for me. I could build stuff with the guys another day. If we didn't do the grapes that night, they'd go to waste. We headed straight home, where we both changed clothes and took our shoes off. "No sense scuffing up good shoes," Momma would say. Though she didn't say it this time, it was a regular habit to take our shoes off and go barefoot until it was too cold outside to go without shoes.

In the shed, Sissy had already pulled off the cheesecloth and was stemming the grapes by the time I arrived. We put aside about half of the grapes to give to Momma and Grandma for making jam. But, we decided to make juice out of the ones in my barrel. Of course, making juice meant smashing the grapes. We could have used Grandma's apple press to get the juice out, but I kept thinking of the pictures on the juice bottles in Mr. Broom's store. The pictures all showed ladies with their skirt tails tucked up into their waistband, smashing grapes with their feet in huge vats. We only had one barrel, not huge vats of grapes. But, we had to do things right, I suggested to Sissy, reminding her of the pictures. She wasn't sure of what I suggested.

She was still shaking her head, not quite convinced, when I got back with a bucket of water from the pump a few minutes later. I didn't want jam to ruin good grape juice. Despite her earlier protests, Sissy smiled and plunged her feet into the cold pump water. Then, I picked her up and stood her in the barrel, kind of like we had done with the sauerkraut. Her lips curled up funny and her smile turned into a look of disgust as the grapes squished between her toes.

"What do I do now?" she asked. "This is awful."

"I'll hold on to keep you from falling," I said. "Start walking in place. Let's try to smash all the juice out as fast as we can before Momma comes out to check on us."

"What do you mean *let's,*" she asked. "I'm the one who's doing the stomping." She began to move her legs up and down as she spoke.

All I could think of was the words I'd heard my Grandma say over and over. "Well, it is *women's work,*" I responded. Then, Sissy reached down and nailed me with a handful of grapes.

About twenty minutes later, the grapes were as smashed as the toes of a young girl could make them. So, I helped Sissy out of the barrel and into the wash water to clean herself off. I put the cheese cloth back over the pulpy mixture of grape skins and juice to keep the bugs out. Then, I started to get Momma and Grandma to share our surprise with them. They could help squeeze the rest of the juice out of the pulp and pour it into containers.

"Michael," my sister sobbed. I looked her way. "It won't come off! My legs are purple!"

I looked. Sure enough, her feet and legs were stained purple by the grape juice. "That's okay, I told her. It'll wash off with Grandma's homemade lye soap later."

That made Sissy feel better. Grandma's soap will eat away at anything. No dirt could survive Grandma's lye soap.

Well, we were right about one thing. Grandma and Momma perked right up when they saw the grapes. It quickly became a family affair, making jam, and making and bottling juice. Momma even called Aunt Anna to come over. She had to have Uncle Alex open the grocery and buy extra sugar. In all the excitement, no one even noticed Sissy's feet and legs. Boy, were they purple!

∿

Late into the night, all burners on the stove were burning blue. Pots had to be stirred constantly. Bottles and jars had to be washed and filled. Work went on throughout the night and into the early hours of the morning. Opportunity didn't present itself like this too often. At one point, Momma kissed me on my forehead as I sat down to close my eyes for a few minutes.

"You're good kids," Momma said to Sissy and me. Sissy had already fallen asleep on the couch. I'd covered her up with a sheet, so no one could see her legs and ruin what was proving to be a happy evening. "But, Michael," Momma continued," Next time, let's do projects like this a little bit at a time."

I woke up in the early morning to see jar after jar of jam lining the counters. Bottles of purple juice made a parade across the background in the kitchen. The whole house smelled of grapes.

"Better get moving, sleepyhead," Momma called to me. "Your sister's already on her way to school."

I groggily put on my knickers and pulled them down over the tops of my long socks. I quickly cleaned up and got ready for school. Then, with a piece of toast covered heavily with the best grape jam I'd ever tasted, I grabbed my books and headed out the door.

I'd gotten almost as far as the shed when I thought I heard a whimpering sound. At first I couldn't tell what it was. I thought maybe an animal had been hurt nearby. When I listened better, however, I recognized the sound as crying. I walked into the shed and saw my sister sitting by the bucket of wash water. Her legs were still stained purple. But, they were blotchy and discolored in places.

Right away, I knew what had happened. My sister had left the house before Momma or Grandma could see her feet and legs. She'd used Grandma's lye soap and scrubbed at the purple until her legs were becoming raw and sore. "It won't come off," she cried, "and I can't go to school like this. All of the kids will laugh at me."

I knew what she said was true. Her anklets only came up about four inches above her shoes. Her purple legs would bring the laughter of everyone as they stood out against her white socks. Then I thought of something! It was too late to go back into the house without admitting to my family what I'd accidentally done to my sister. But I could remedy my mistake. I took off my own shoes and socks. I handed my knee socks to Sissy and pulled my shoes back onto my bare feet. I looked goofy, but at least my sister could hide the purple.

I wiped away Sissy's tears. I even carried her books for her, that is until we got close to school, but then, I gave them back. Lots of the guys teased me for going without my socks that day, but not one person noticed my sister's purple feet.

CHAPTER 14

SINK HOLE DISASTER

THE BIG NEWS OF THE WEEK came when the sheriff interrupted school one morning. He was looking for John Edward Branshuk. We'd noticed that he wasn't in school, but that wasn't so odd. Everyone got sick once in awhile, including the banker's son. When we saw the sheriff, I was sure John Edward was in trouble for tearing down the company bridge and stealing building material. Right away, I was glad that I hadn't joined the others with their project. They hadn't asked me back since that first time.

We all pretended to do our work while we strained to hear what the Sheriff said to Mrs. Honniger in the hall. When the two of them came into the room, we got another surprise. The Sheriff had left his wide-brimmed hat on while out in the hall, but took it off with one hand as he opened the door for our teacher and followed her quietly into the room. We watched, pretty impressed that our teacher could even make the Sheriff take off his hat before entering the room.

"Boys and girls," Mrs. Honniger started, "The Sheriff has an important question to ask all of you." Then, she stepped back from her usual place at the front of the classroom and let the Sheriff take over.

"You all know John Branshuk," he began. I looked around and saw everyone shaking their heads up and down, waiting to hear more.

"You mean, John Edward Branshuk," came a nasal sounding voice from the back of the room. I turned around just quick enough to see Tommy Sapinski's nose up in the air, giving his John Edward impression. Several other students also caught his actions and began to giggle. A glance from Mrs. Honniger, however, quickly restored order to the room.

The Sheriff took advantage of the silence and resumed his talk. "I need to know if any of you have seen John Edward Branshuk." Then, he looked back at Tommy, who already had his hand in the air.

"Why? Is he in trouble?" asked Tommy, hopefully. Tommy and John Edward had had a difference of opinion a few days earlier. The scuffle that followed left Tommy with a black eye and a distaste for John Edward Branshuk and his stuck up ways.

To Tommy's disappointment, the Sheriff shook his head no. "No, he's not in trouble with the law, if that's what you mean. But, he might be in some other kind of trouble. He didn't come home the night before last and hasn't been seen since."

The whole room was silent. For the first time, we began to realize the seriousness of the sheriff's presence. My mind raced through everything that had could have happened. The possibilities were endless; most of them didn't fit John Edward Branshuk. He wasn't the type to get adventurous and run away. Plus, no one would want to take him.

Conversations broke out spontaneously all over the room. "What if…?" were the most frequently heard words. Then, when everyone realized that none of the varieties of explanations for his disappearance could be true, the room became silent once again. Everyone stared at the Sheriff and waited until he spoke.

"It's probably nothing to worry about, he said, but I want everyone of you to go straight home from school tonight and stay there. We'll have teams of volunteers searching everywhere in the bottoms. Until we find out what happened to John Edward, we don't want to take the chance of someone else coming up missing."

A few of the girls began to cry, because that's what they knew was expected of them. Mrs. Honniger passed out tissues. The fellows just sat in stony silence, each wishing that he could be the object of everyone's attention like John Edward Branshuk was at that time.

The Sheriff excused himself, and Mrs. Honniger tried to teach us long division and uncommon verb tenses, but our hearts weren't in our work. Math and parts of speech couldn't compete with the mystery of John Edward Branshuk's disappearance. Eventually, Mrs. Honniger gave up trying to teach and gave us time to read independently for the rest of the day.

The dismissal bell started all the "What if…?" conversations up again. Nobody had answers to the questions. The school grounds cleared out quickly that day. Everyone hurried home to tell their families of the latest news. I walked home with Sissy as usual, and we talked along the way.

"Maybe he ran off to join the circus," said Sissy. "Or maybe, he went to join the Foreign Legion."

"I know he didn't run off to join anything," I said back to her. "He isn't the type to be out after dark. He doesn't even like to run through the bottoms with the rest of us, because he's afraid that something might get him."

"Then maybe a hobo got him," she said in a worried voice. "Grandma says there's lots of hoboes around here."

I remembered my one experience with the 'bo who had saved

me from the snake and decided quickly that there was no chance that a hobo would do anything like take a child. We didn't have a solution by the time we got home. As we walked through the door, Sissy took over watching Gertie from our Momma, whose face held a pleading expression..

"Do something with this sister of yours," Momma said to Sissy, or young Mr. Branshuk won't be the only child missing." We wondered how Momma knew about the disappearance, but decided right then wasn't the time to ask. It was obvious that Gertie or something had driven Momma to the brink today. Sissy responded by taking Gertie by the hand and leading her out to the shed for a wagon ride. "And, Michael Andrew Polonec, I want you to take this infernal dog for a walk." She handed me Pal's leash. I wondered what could have happened to make Momma so upset that she was using my whole name!

"Don't you call my dog names while you're living under this roof," I heard Grandma say from the other room in a stern voice to Momma. I looked up at Momma's face and saw that her eyes were red. She shook her head with that 'Don't you dare ask!' look on her face, and then turned to walk away.

Before going out the door with Pal, I walked over to the cupboard and opened the cookie jar for my usual handful of homemade cookies. My hand came out empty. So I reached in deeper, yet I still found no cookies. I did find something else, however. An official looking note lay on the counter next to the cookie jar. I started to read it, then thought better as I heard Momma coming back. Pal and I headed out the door in a hurry. All I had caught was a few phrases like, "back interest due" and "mortgage to be foreclosed." Then, I pieced it together as I walked toward Pal's spot in the bottoms. Momma must have gotten a letter about the farm. She must have gone to check it out at the bank. That's probably where she heard about John Edward, I decided. With the mystery about Momma's anger solved in my mind, I started to think about John Edward's disappearance.

"Snort!" went Pal. I let him off his leash to chase a rabbit. As I watched him tear through the brush, I wondered why Momma had put the leash on him in the first place. Pal never had to be on a leash unless we were going downtown or somewhere where we had to walk Pal on the sidewalk. Suddenly, a thought hit me. *Just as Pal didn't like to stay on a sidewalk, John Edward Branshuk wouldn't go through anywhere that was the least bit rough or overgrown.*

⌒

I was sure the search party would be looking over by the company bridge, where John Edward was headed that night. But, he wouldn't have walked through the bottoms like the rest of us fellows would, even if it was the shortest way to get there. I called Pal and headed for the old tracks on the long way around town. Though the tracks weren't in use, the trees and brush were cut way back, making a clearing. That had to be the way he would have gone, if he'd gone to the bridge the night he came up missing.

Pal followed me grudgingly back up the hill. He wanted to spend more time sniffing around the bottoms, and wasn't anxious to go home yet. He was a little happier when we passed by the house and headed for the old tracks. I walked along the tracks with my eyes opened wide as Pal put his nose to the ground and wandered back and forth. I kept my eyes and ears open as I walked along, sure that if anything unusual was there that Pal and I would spot it.

Suddenly, Pal tore past me, snorting and drooling as he ran. He stopped in the middle of the tracks, maybe thirty or forty yards ahead of where I walked. He stuck his head down for a moment between two tracks and stood still. As I walked closer, he lifted up his head and let loose with a mournful howl. It was a howl I had not heard since I had found him at Grandpa's feet, the day Grandpa had died.

For several minutes, I didn't come any closer, afraid of what I might find. Pal put his head between the tracks again and started to dig. I got mad. That stupid dog wasn't looking for John Edward. He'd found a rabbit hole! I walked closer, ready to scold him… Until I saw that the hole was too big for a rabbit. *Must be a fox den or something like that,* I thought.

Then, I noticed that the hole was way too big to be a den of any kind. Besides, no animal would dig between the tracks themselves. I walked over to where Pal was digging, trying to get at whatever was down there. As I approached, I saw the ground start to sink beneath Pal's hind legs, and he began to disappear from view. I dove forward, landing on my belly and my elbows, catching him by the collar just before he slipped entirely into the hole. The sudden weight of the fat little dog caused my arms to scrape forward over the white, angular rocks that served as ballast between the tracks and rails.

Despite the pain from the rocks that cut into my bare arms, I pulled Pal out of the hole, and eased myself backwards. I sat down and held him in my arms while I caught my breath. Pal snorted gratefully and washed my face with his tongue. Next, he began to treat my wounds. He licked the blood off of my cuts as I pulled pieces of rock and gravel out of my open scrapes. Each of us satisfied that the other was okay, Pal and I both stepped back to inspect the hole.

"What in the world could cause such a thing?" I wondered out loud to myself. "What would cause a hole to sink like that?" As I spoke the words softly, the answer came to me, *"sinkhole!"*

Grandpa had taught me about sinkholes. When the miners dug our areas of coal, they shored up the mines with timbers. In places where they didn't use enough timber to hold up the mine, or where ground water had helped to rot out the timbers, parts of the mines had been known to collapse, causing sinkholes. Some holes went down only a few feet—others went down *hundreds of feet*. Grandpa said the hole at the surface level would be small. But, the hole mushroomed out as it went deeper. Something that fell through a sinkhole at the top could end up blocks away as it tumbled down through the interlocking system of mines.

My mind stopped thinking about mining and went back to thinking about John Edward Branshuk. A terrible thought raced through my mind, and I turned to run and find the Sheriff and Mr. Branshuk, the banker.

Pal and I left the tracks and headed straight through the brush. Tired and scratched up from wild raspberry canes, I reached the bottoms and headed for the company bridge. I could hear the hounds baying in the distance. The sounds led me to where the volunteer search party scoured the woods and area all around the river bottoms. Out of breath, I stood panting, among the group of bewildered men, trying to get enough air to talk.

"I thought the Sheriff told all of you kids to stay home." said an arrogant voice. "You're in the way. Get out of here, now!"

I looked to where the voice had come from and recognized the face of the town banker, Mr. Branshuk, John Edward's father himself.

"I think I might ..." I began, but I was cut off.

"I don't care what you think," he shouted, drowning out what I had to say, and then he grabbed me by the elbow and started to shove me back towards home. His grip put pressure on my fresh scrape, and I winced in pain. That's when Pal came running into the clearing. With his short legs flying, he leaped trough the air to Mr. Branshuk, who still held his master. He grabbed Mr. Branshuk by the pant leg and growled menacingly.

The Sheriff and everyone else came running. One of the deputies pulled out his pistol and pointed it at Pal.

"No!" I screamed. Then Pal let go and blew snot all over the banker's feet.

Not one person moved. Everyone stopped in their tracks. No one dared to laugh or to say a word. Not even one of the hounds made a sound.

I took advantage of the silence. "Mr. Branshuk," I said, "I'm sorry for what Pal just did, but I think I know where your son is." The banker, who usually stood tall before everyone, now slumped his shoulders in shame for displaying such anger toward me earlier. A tear ran down his cheek as he waited for me to say more.

❧

When the Sheriff heard about the possibility that John Edward had fallen into a sinkhole, he ordered his deputies to head that way with their hounds. Mrs. Branshuk had sent a volunteer over with one of John Edward's shirts after a request of the Sheriff. The deputies gave each hound a fresh smell of the shirt and headed for the place I had described. Not more than a few minutes later, we heard the excited howls of hounds on a trail. As fast as we could go, the Sheriff, Mr. Branshuk, Pal and I went through the brush following the sounds.

Anyone who has ever heard a coon hound on a hunt would recognize the sound we heard a few minutes later. Loud baying could be heard across the river bottoms. The hounds were on the trail! We arrived in minutes to find deputies straining to keep the hounds from ripping the hole open further. Everyone knew that digging at the hole now could cause rubble to fall on John Edward. If he was still alive, some other way would have to be found to get at him than to dig from the surface.

One of the volunteers used to work in the mines. "It's no use," he said. That's more than a short drop. The mine under here goes clear down to the bottoms. It's a deep one. You'd never be able to dig the boy up in time from the surface, and all the mine entrances have been sealed shut for years. It would take days to even get into the mines, let alone to find the boy. I'm afraid it's hopeless."

Around the circle of men, heads hung sadly. All eyes were on the Sheriff, as they waited to hear him say the words they knew must come, that it was too late—that everyone should go home. Mr. Branshuk stood with his arms around his wife who was whimpering and gasping for breath. The two of them were trying to comfort each other. I tried to get close enough to talk to them, but the deputies made me keep my distance.

Then, I saw my father coming down the tracks. In all the excitement, I hadn't checked in at home. I didn't know whether Papa had heard about what had happened or if Momma had sent him out to search for me. It didn't matter. I had something to say, and I knew the one person who could get everyone to listen was my Papa. I quickly explained about the sinkhole to him and told him about the problem getting into the mines with all the entrances sealed up. I confessed to him about my secret place and my close call the day Grandpa had died.

My Papa scooped me up and hugged me. Then he put me down and forced his way through the crowd. He went straight for the Sheriff and Mr. Branshuk. The next thing I knew, Pal and I were in the front seat of a speeding squad car, the envy of every boy in town. The siren screamed as the squad car raced straight for Grandma's house at the top of the bottoms.

Gertie sat clapping her hands as Sissy—pulling her in the wagon— came to find out what on earth was happening. Momma and Grandma came out onto the porch in their aprons, leaving supper preparations behind in the kitchen. Deputies and volunteers all followed Pal and me as we led them all down the path to my secret spot. I pointed out the location, and my secret spot ceased to be a secret.

Men with flashlights and hurricane lamps crawled through the tight opening that had been made for the a small boy. It seems as though they hauled miles of ropes in with them, all tied end to end. Everyone going in used the ropes as a lifeline to find their way back out. After years of neglect in the mines, no maps could be used accurately to find one's way back out if someone got lost. Men going off in different branches of the mine attached their ropes to the main trunk line to find their way back to the entrance later. Several of the men held the leashes of their hounds, afraid to let the hounds run ahead without them.

Then, all of the excitement seemed to stop. With most of the men inside the mine, the rest of us stood outside hoping and praying that John Edward would be found. Father Zarecki arrived and stooped, saying the Rosary with Mrs. Branshuk who sat on a fallen tree trunk. It didn't matter to her that she wasn't Catholic. It comforted her as she listened to him repeat the prayers and move the glistening prayer beads through his hands. Momma crossed herself as she walked by the priest. She came up and planted a wet messy kiss on my forehead and stood beside me. I didn't even mind that she did it in public.

After what seemed to be the longest time, we saw the first of many lights coming back towards the entrance to my not-so-secret spot. Mrs. Branshuk's eyes were on the Sheriff as he came out of the opening empty handed. Her head dropped, and she started crying. Mr. Branshuk came out, also empty handed. It was the first time I'd ever seen the banker dirty and looking haggard. His wife saw him and began to shake all over as she sobbed. But then, Mr. Branshuk turned around, reaching back into the opening, where a pair of strong arms held his son. He carried the limp body toward his wife, who peeked out through her fingers. I don't think anybody breathed until and the hint of a smile started to form across the banker's face. After allowing ourselves to take a long breath, we all saw John Edward Branshuk blink his eyes as the sunlight touched his face for the first time in two days.

"Tired and hungry," said the Sheriff to everyone. "But, other than that, he's all right."

A cheer went up from all the searchers—tentative at first, but growing to a sound that filled the bottoms. Then Father Zarecki led us all in a prayer of thanks.

CHAPTER 15

DOIN' WHAT'S RIGHT ISN'T ALWAYS EASY

"AND A LITTLE CHILD SHALL LEAD THEM...." said the voice of Father Zarecki the next day in a special Mass at church. Momma looked over at me with pride in her eyes. This was a different look than she had on her face when I explained how I'd known about the entrance to the mine. She'd cried as if I had been the one who had been lost in the mine. Of course, not too long ago, I had been.

Right away after I'd told her the whole story, Momma made me promise on the family Bible that I would never play in the mines again. That would be an easy promise to keep. One scare like that in a lifetime was going to be enough for me. Then, she made me go to confession, to tell the priest everything I'd told her.

I had dragged my heels all the way to St. Edwards. I was not terribly excited about telling the dirt to Father Zarecki and having him lecture me. But, to my surprise, confession hadn't been too bad. The priest was more interested in the details of the rescue than in making me pray to God for forgiveness. Now, as I listened to him talk, he was using what I'd told him to give the homily, or sermon as my non-Catholic friends called it.

"Out of the darkness and into the light," echoed Father Zarecki's voice through the church. "And a little child shall lead the way!"

I think he was really talking about God, but it felt like all eyes were on me whenever he used the words "little child." I didn't like being called a little child in the homily, but I had to admit that it was pretty nice that everyone in Coalton knew how I'd helped John Edward get out of the mine alive. They all made me feel pretty special. Even Mary Jane Bronatto was looking at me from across the aisle. And she was smiling.

She looked at me for a long moment. She looked up the aisle and then at the front of the church towards the altar. Then back at me. I looked at where she sat and then followed her glances around the church. My mind started working. If I timed it just right, I could get out into the aisle right next to her and we could walk side by side to the altar to receive communion at the same time. I had to admit, I was one pretty sly fellow. Mary Jane Bronatto was the catch of my sixth grade class.

Father Zarecki finished the homily. The ushers were moving back row by row, allowing people to step into the aisle for the walk to the front. I edged over towards the aisle. Mary Jane did the same. The ushers were now at the row ahead of me. Mary Jane stood up and smiled at me.

I started to rise, and then I felt a hand on my shoulder. My Grandma, who had been sitting in the pew behind me pressed me back into my seat momentarily, while she stepped out into the aisle before it was her turn and headed for the front—walking right beside Mary Jane Bronatto, leaving me to walk beside Mary Jane's Mother. My love life was ruined by a Grandma who believed that Mass was a place for worshipping God, not girls.

It was when we walked out of Mass later that a series of odd events made me quickly forget about Mary Jane. John Edward Branshuk's father was standing outside as we exited. This alone was odd, because as I said before, he wasn't Catholic. I guess he knew where we'd be and had come to find my Father. He caught Papa's attention and called him to one side, while the rest of us headed for the family car.

Momma's eyes were on the two of them the entire time they talked. Though it was only a brief conversation, it seemed as if they talked for hours. Mr. Branshuk tried to hand Papa an envelope, but Papa raised both hands, palms facing Mr. Branshuk as if to push the envelope away. He kept shaking his head from side to side, saying no to whatever Mr. Branshuk had to say. Then, Papa left the obviously disappointed banker and headed back towards the car with his head held high. Mr. Branshuk stood with one hand holding the envelope at his side, while scratching his head with the other hand.

Papa got into the car, started the engine, and headed for Main Street. We had to take Uncle Alex, Anna, and the baby home before returning to Grandma's house at the top of the bottoms. The silence was loud in the car. Everyone wanted to know what the banker said to Papa, but no one asked. I wanted to know what was in that envelope, too. Momma, in particular, focused her eyes on Papa, burning a hole in the side of his head with her glare.

The only words exchanged during the ride home came from Papa to Uncle Alex when we dropped them off at the store. "I'll be back after I take everyone home. We need to talk!"

I watched Uncle Alex climb out of the front seat from next to Momma and open the back door for Aunt Anna and the baby. We all breathed again as we slid over, now that we had room to move. Uncle Alex used his key to open the front door of the grocery store, walking through the store to the back to take his family upstairs.

∾

As we pulled away from the curb, I couldn't help but think about how much things had changed in just a few months. It was a lot different than when I'd first walked Aunt Anna around the block to the back alley to get home.

Those thoughts left my mind in a hurry as Gertie climbed over me, trying to get Momma's attention. When she didn't get a response, Gertie climbed over the seat and wiggled onto Momma's lap. Momma looked sternly at Sissy since Sissy had let Gertie go from her own lap, where Gertie had been when we were tightly packed together for the ride home from Mass.

We reached home and Papa shut off the engine after pulling into the driveway. With his foot on the clutch, he shifted the car into neutral and let the silent car glide up to the house.

Everyone piled out. Led by Grandma, we walked up the steps and through the kitchen door. Grandma walked straight to the kitchen drawer next to the ice box where she kept her apron and put it on. The three of us kids went to change out of our good clothes into something more comfortable. Even Gertie knew better than to leave her Sunday best on, especially since the special Mass had been held on a Saturday. If it had been Sunday, Momma probably would have put on her apron and joined Grandma in the kitchen. As I walked up the stairs, however, I saw her standing—feet apart and hands on her hips—watching Papa walk through the kitchen on his way into the den.

Curiosity got the best of me. I carried my clothes back downstairs on the double. I wanted to see the fireworks between my silent Papa and my determined Momma. My plan was to watch the action while I changed. Papa had headed straight for Grandma's old desk. He pulled up the rolltop front and reached into the compartment at the top left. I knew that's where he kept important family papers. Momma knew the same and wasn't about to watch silently any more.

I tucked my shirt into my pants as I shadowed Momma who was following Papa back through the kitchen and out of the screen door. I was smart enough, however, to remain inside and do my listening through the screen.

"Exactly what is going on between you and the bank, and, why are you going to talk to Alex before you talk to me?" It was more than hurt from being left out of something that I heard in her voice. There was a sound of anger that scared me! Momma used a tone of voice that she reserved for only the most serious of occasions.

"Momma," Papa said, "I know what you want and what you will ask me to do, if I tell you. And I just can't do it. It isn't right!" He turned abruptly and started for the car. This was unusual, to see my Papa acting this way towards Momma. He usually let her have her way in nearly everything. This wasn't like him. I didn't understand what was going on.

"He offered you the farm. Didn't he," Momma said through clenched teeth.

Papa opened the car door.

"You answer me!" she shouted. Then, she grabbed the car door as Papa got in and kept it from closing.

"That's right!" Papa answered. "He offered me the farm."

"You know how badly I want a home of our own," Momma shot back. She stood back, letting go of the car. Momma took out her kerchief and brought it to her eyes. At this, Papa got back out of the car and put both of his large hands on Momma's shoulders.

Looking her in the eyes, he said, "It isn't right. You don't save people's lives for profit. Michael did what was right. He did it because it was the right thing to do. What kind of message will it give to him and to every other person in town, if we accept that kind of payment for doing what people are supposed to do for each other? Momma, I love you, but I can't accept the farm like that. Would you want to live with me if I didn't have my pride?" He stood there silent and waited for a reply.

Hearing my name and hearing my Father speak of his affection for my Mother suddenly made me feel embarrassed for listening in on what was meant to be a private conversation. But, when I turned around to leave, I bumped into Gertie, Sissy, and Grandma. All three were stacked up behind me, leaning forward, one head above the other. We almost all went down like dominoes. Even Pal sat on the top, trying to hear what was going on. Since it seemed like the popular thing to do, I turned around to listen once more.

"If I don't have anything to say about this, why are you going to talk to Alex?" Momma asked in a hurt tone of voice. She had her back to Papa and refused to look at him while he answered.

"I … I mean we, can only decide what's right for us. It's not right to keep Alex from having a chance to get the farm back, if that's really what he wants. "It's just not right to take advantage of other people just because they feel like they owe you for something God would want us to do. Do you think it's easy to give up a possible chance to get back on our feet?" I could hear a choking in Daddy's voice as the words came out when he continued. "Doin' what's right isn't always easy."

When Momma didn't respond, he closed the car door and started the car. Momma finally turned around as the car finished backing out of the driveway and wiped the tears from her eyes. She turned back towards the house. That was the signal for everyone to move. Sissy grabbed Gertie by the hand and ran back through the kitchen to head out the front door, stopping only long enough to swipe a piece of bread for each to chew on. Both recognized it might be a long time before we ate.

Grandma began to rummage through the cupboards, making a lot of noise, and Pal started to scratch at the door, the signal that he wanted to go for a walk. Quickly deciding that Pal had a good idea, I opened the door, and the two of us ran past Momma before she could ask where we were going.

We headed straight for Mr. Brovotsky's Grocery downtown. I decided that Pal needed a bone to chew on, and what place could possibly be better. Amazingly enough, when we got there, Papa's car was sitting out in front. Pal waited for me while I went inside. I saw Papa in the back talking to Uncle Alex. Though I was dying to know what was being said, I kept my distance and walked straight towards the meat counter.

"I haven't seen you for a while," said Mr. Brovotsky. It was hard to think of him as Mr. Brooms nowadays. He no longer shook his broom in anger whenever kids came around. Since Uncle Alex had come to work for him, he acted friendly towards everyone.

"I wanted to know if you have a bone I can have for Pal," I blurted out. "I'd really appreciate it."

"Certainly, young man," said Mr. Brovotsky. He reached into the barrel behind the meat counter and took out a huge bone, wrapped it in brown butcher paper, and tied a string around it. This certainly wasn't the same man who would have taken my head off for asking for anything free a few short months ago.

I thanked Mr. Brovotsky and headed outside to my waiting pet. I bent down and scratched Pal between the ears while I waited for Papa. Pal slobbered all over the sidewalk as he sniffed at the wrapped package I held in my hands.

"Michael," a voice behind me said. I recognized it as Papa's and turned around. There he stood, waiting for me to stand up, which I promptly did. "You know what's been happening, don't you?"

"I'm not totally sure what's happening," I honestly replied. Then I began to match strides beside him as he indicated that he wanted to walk. "I know Mr. Branshuk offered you something because his son was saved, and that you turned it down. I also know that Momma's madder than I've ever seen her," I added.

"That's most of it," he agreed. "But there's more. First, we just can't take a handout for something you did to help save the banker's son. Not only do I believe that it's wrong, but Mr. Branshuk doesn't have the authority to do what he wanted to do. The money in the bank isn't just his. It belongs to everyone in this town. If we let him give the farm to us, everyone in this town could be hurt. Your Momma wants her own house so bad, and I want to give it to her. But, I can't explain all of this to her. The words just won't come out right."

Listening to Papa made me realize why so many men acted like they had to be the head of the family in all decisions. They just didn't feel secure enough to share decisions, or were worried their pride might suffer if they had to give an explanation with a decision. As we walked, I decided that I was proud of my Papa and the way he led his life. He always showed respect for others. He wouldn't take what wasn't his.

I just hoped he could get Momma to understand his decision— or that the two could decide it together.

We'd circled several blocks before arriving back at the car. Then, the two of us with Pal got into the car and headed for Grandma's. Once we got home, we went inside. Dinner was waiting on the table, but it was cold. Not only was the food cold, but so was the reception Papa received from Momma. She wouldn't even talk to him, preferring to stand at the cupboard rather than even sit at the same table.

Papa ignored her silence and began to talk about his conversation with Uncle Alex. The last thing Momma wanted to hear was that Uncle Alex had accepted the farm that Papa had turned down. She wanted that farmhouse for her family. She could smell the bread baking in her very own kitchen and hear her husband cleaning his boots after a long day behind the plow!

What came next wasn't what I expected, or feared.

Momma looked surprised, but relieved when Papa said that Alex would not accept the farm either. Still silent, but more interested in listening at that point, Momma poured Papa a cup of coffee from the blue porcelain pot and sat down. I decided I'd better leave the two of them to talk out their problems and fixed myself a sandwich to eat outside. As I was leaving, I heard Papa tell her the speech he'd practiced on me as we'd walked together. I was pretty happy that I'd been able to help a little bit at getting them to talk to each other.

The rest of that day and night went pretty well. There wasn't much conversation around the house. But, at least everyone was friendly as we sat around the radio listening to our favorite programs like we did every Saturday night.

"And a mighty Hi Ho Silver, the Lone Ranger rides again!!" The familiar voice of the announcer brought a feeling of comfort to us all, despite all of the problems from earlier in the day. Grandma laughed with us kids during part of the programs. Then, we all sat quietly as President Hoover came across the radio waves telling us all that life was going to get better. You couldn't have guessed it by the look on Momma's face, though. She still sat there, troubled.

Then, the radio fell silent. When we all got up to head for bed, Pal's ears perked up, as if he heard something. The sounds of tires could be heard crunching on the gravel driveway. Then came the sound of a car door opening and closing, followed by footsteps up the steps and onto the porch. There was a long minute of silence, before a knock at the door could be heard by everyone. We all stood watching as Papa walked toward the door.

Grandma put on her glasses and pulled her robe tighter around her middle. Sissy picked up Gertie and held her. Momma sat without showing any signs of curiosity, beyond caring for the moment who it might be. I walked with Papa to open the door, curious to see who it was at this time of the night.

Papa opened the door and, after exchanging greetings, invited the caller inside. It was Mr. Branshuk again. Now, Momma perked up expressing an interest in what Papa and Mr. Branshuk had to say to one another.

"I've thought about what you said," stated Mr. Branshuk. "You were right. Your son didn't save my boy for personal gain. I was wrong to try and pay you for my son's life." He stood there looking at Papa with an intense look on his face. "I'm just used to everyone needing money so bad, with the depression and all, that I thought that might be that best way to help you. I know you didn't help us to make a profit, and I don't want to hurt your pride. But, I do want to help you in some way if I can. How would it be if I work with the bank in Wisconsin to give you more time on the lien for the farm? That way, you won't lose the farm. The bank won't be out big money. And I can do something that lets you know how grateful my wife and I are." He stood there in front of all of us with a pleading look on his face.

I looked at Papa. Then, we both looked at Momma. She had a pleading look on her face, too.

"We'll talk it over with each other and with my brother and his wife," Papa said to Mr. Branshuk. If it's okay, we'll stop by the bank on Monday and give you our decision. Regardless of what we decide, we're grateful for the offer," said Papa and shook his hand. Then, he walked Mr. Branshuk back out to his car.

Grandma put the girls to bed. I looked at Momma again as I rose to go upstairs. She looked at me contentedly, so I knew I'd done the right thing by getting up to leave the room. Some big decisions would have to be made by Momma and Papa that affected all of us, and they didn't need me in the road.

Momma lit an extra candle before Mass the next morning. It seemed strange to go to church two days in a row, but it was nice to see Momma speaking to Papa again. Grandma had stayed home from Mass to start her special chicken for everyone. She was browning the crust and peeling potatoes as we left for church.

When we arrived home, the crispy brown pieces of chicken were baking in the oven and Grandma was stirring her special gravy.

"You can't make important decisions on an empty stomach," Grandma said, as she put the first piece of chicken on Papa's plate. "Now, eat first, then talk." So, that's just what everyone did.

By the end of the afternoon, it was all decided. Both Uncle Alex and Papa agreed that it made sense to accept the offer of extra time to pay off the bank loan and that it wouldn't be charity to accept such an offer. Momma cringed when Papa gave Uncle Alex the choice of whether or not he wanted to return to the farm. I knew what she was thinking, "Of course Uncle Alex will want to resume his farming explorations!"

But we were all surprised when Uncle Alex turned down the offer.

It seems Mr. Brovotsky had offered Uncle Alex a partnership in the store. The old man had said he said he felt like Uncle Alex made up in some way for his son who had died so far away from home. Uncle Alex told Papa about his unexpected joy at repairing things for people around town. He said, "Giving new life to a radio seems like a small thing, but it gives me a lot of satisfaction to make it work again when I know the family needs that radio to hear their favorite weekly programs. I can't be the Lone Ranger, but I can make it possible for him to visit a humble home." So, Uncle Alex turned down the chance to take over the family farm once again.

Momma looked anxiously at Papa. Instead of telling her what he thought they should do, Papa asked Momma for her opinion. Momma immediately said she wanted the chance to move to *her own home* on the farm in Wisconsin.

Grandma looked hurt, she didn't want to be alone anymore now that Grandpa was gone. She had grown accustomed to the sound of family in her house.

But, her eyes had no sooner fallen, it seemed, than she perked up. Her sadness lasted for only a moment. Uncle Alex added one more piece of news to the conversation. Aunt Anna was pregnant. Alex and Anna would have to find a bigger place to live. Besides, the increase in business at the store meant the apartment above the store would be needed for storage. Grandma felt better when everyone decided that Uncle Alex and his expanding family should live with her.

Momma brightened up when it was decided that we would move to Wisconsin to take over the family farm. She would have a house of her own again. Each of us kids would have our own room, and we would get a chance to live on the farm we'd heard so many stories about. The only sad part in the whole decision process was that Pal would remain at his home with Grandma. He belonged in the home he'd known for so many years, the house at the top of the bottoms.

If you have enjoyed this book, point your browser to:

www.mikelockett.com

www.parkhurstbrothers.com

www.storynet.org